THE ALIEN WAS A CAN OF WORMS

It was a horror, Jason Whitney thought. Some of them weren't bad; others of them were. This was the worst he had ever seen.

He started to put out his mind cautiously, then pulled back. He had to settle down before he tried to talk with this thing. The alien reached out and touched him with a mental probe.

—Welcome, it said, to this snug retreat. You are a human creature.

—Yes, Jason said. This is the planet Earth.

—That is the designation. I was sure when I arrived that it was a proper planet, the one of the traveler I communicated very far ago.

—You mean you sought our Earth? You aren't simply stopping off to rest?

—I came to seek a soul, the alien said. The traveler told me that humans had once had souls and might still have, and I say to myself, so wonderful a thing is worth the seeking of. Do you have a soul?

Also by Clifford D. Simak
Published by Ballantine Books:

MASTODONIA

THE FELLOWSHIP OF TALISMAN

THE VISITORS

WAY STATION

PROJECT POPE

A CHOICE OF GODS

Clifford D. Simak

A Del Rey Book

BALLANTINE BOOKS • NEW YORK

A Del Rey Book
Published by Ballantine Books

Copyright © 1972 by Clifford D. Simak

Library of Congress Catalog Card Number: 78-171472

ISBN 0-345-29868-3

This edition published in hardcover by G. P. Putnam's Sons.

Manufactured in the United States of America

First Ballantine Books Edition: February 1982

Cover art by Ralph Brillhart

1

Aug. 1, 2185: So we begin again. Actually, we began again fifty years ago, but did not know it then. There was hope, for a time, that there were more people left and that we could pick up where we had left off. We thought, somehow, that we could hang onto what we had, once the shock was over and we could think more clearly and plan more cleverly. By the end of the first year we should have known that it was impossible; by the end of five we should have been willing to admit it, but we weren't. At first we refused to face the fact and once we had to face it we became stubborn with a senseless sort of faith. The old way of life could not be revived; there were too few of us and none with special knowledge and the old technology was gone beyond all restoration. The technology had been too complex and too specialized and too regimented to be picked up and carried on without a large work force equipped with appropriate skills and knowledge that were necessary not only to operate the technology itself, but to produce the energy that went into it. We are now no more than scavengers feeding on the carcass of the past and some day we'll be down to the bare bones of it and will be finally on our own. But over the years we have been recovering or rediscovering,

whichever it may be, some of the older and more
basic technology geared to a simpler way of life and
these basic rudimentary skills should keep us from
sinking into utter savagery.

There is no one who knows what really happened,
which does not, of course, deter some of us from
formulating theories that might explain it all. The
trouble is that all the theories boil down to simple
guesses, in which all kinds of metaphysical miscon-
ceptions play a part. There are no facts other than
two very simple facts and the first of these is that
fifty years ago last month the greater fraction of the
human race either went somewhere or was taken
somewhere. Out of more than eight billion of us,
which was certainly far too many of us, there are
now, at most, a few hundred left. In this house in
which I sit to write these words, there are sixty-seven
humans, and only that many because on the night
it happened we had invited some young guests to
help us celebrate the coming of age of our twin
grandsons, John and Jason Whitney. Of the Leech
Lake Indians there may be as many as three hundred, although we now see little of them, for they
have taken up again, quite happily and to their great
advantage, or so it would seem to me, their old
tribal wanderings. At times rumors reach us of other
little pockets of humanity still surviving (the rumors
chiefly brought by some loose-footed robot), but
when we've gone to hunt for them, they are never
there, nor is there anything to indicate they ever had
been there. This, of course, proves nothing. It stands
to reason that elsewhere on the Earth there must be
others left, although we have no idea where. We hunt
for them no longer, even when the rumors come, for
it seems to us that we no longer have any need of
them. In the intervening years we have become content, settling down into the routine of a bucolic life.

The robots still are with us and we have no idea
how many there may be. All the robots that were

ever in existence must still remain. They did not go or were not taken as was the human race. Over the years a number of them have come to settle in with us, doing all the work and chores necessary for our comfortable existence, becoming, in all truth, a part of our community. Some of them at times may leave and go elsewhere for a while and there are occasions when new ones float in and stay, either for good or for varying periods. It might seem to someone unacquainted with the situation that in the robots we had the labor force we needed to keep at least a small sector of the more vital parts of the old technology alive. It is possible the robots could have been taught the necessary skills, but the rub here is that we had no one who was equipped to teach them. Even if we'd had, I have some well-founded doubt that it would have worked. The robots are not technologically minded. They were not built to be. They were built to bolster human vanity and pride, to meet a strange longing that seems to be built into the human ego—the need to have other humans (or a reasonable facsimile of other humans) to minister to our wants and needs, human slaves to be dominated, human beings over which a man or woman (or a child) can assert authority, thus building up a false feeling of superiority. They were built to serve as cooks, gardeners, butlers, maids, footmen (I have never got quite straight in mind what a footman is)—servants of all kinds. They were the flunkeys and the inferior companions, the yea-sayers, the slaves. In a manner of speaking, in their services to us, I suppose they still are slaves. Although I doubt the robots think of it as slavery; their values, while supplied by human agency, are not entirely human values. They serve us most willingly; thankful of a chance to serve, they press their services upon us, apparently glad to find new masters to replace the old. This is the situation as it applies to us; with the Indians it is different. The robots do not feel at ease with the Indians and the Indians, in turn, regard them with an emotion that borders upon loathing. They are a part of the white man's culture and are readily acceptable to us upon the basis of our one-time preoccupation with machines. To the Indians they are unclean, something that is repulsively foul and alien. They will have no part of them. Any robot stumbling into an Indian camp is summarily hustled off. A few of the robots serve us. There must be many thousands more. Those that are not with us we have fallen into the habit of calling wild robots, although I doubt they, in any sense, are wild. Often, from our windows or while sitting on the patio, or while out walking, we see bands of wild robots hurrying along as if they had an urgent destination or were involved in some great purpose. We have never been able to determine where the destination or what might be the purpose. There are certain stories of them that we hear at times, but nothing more than stories and with no evidence, and not worth repeating here.

I said there were two facts and then got lost in the telling of the first. This is the second fact: Our lives are much longer now. In some strange way which no one pretends to understand, the process of aging, if not halted, has been slowed. I have not seemed to age at all, nor have any of the others, in these last fifty years. If there are a few more white hairs I cannot detect them; if I walk a little slower after fifty years I am not aware of it. I was sixty then and I still am sixty. The youngsters develop to maturity in the usual manner and the normal course of time, but once they reach maturity, the aging seems to stop. Our twin grandsons, whose twenty-first birthday we observed fifty years ago, still are twenty-one. They are, to all physical appearances, the same age as their sons and their oldest grandsons and at times this becomes somewhat disconcerting to someone like myself, who has lived his

entire life with aging, and with the expectation of it.
But disconcerting as it may be, I do not quibble with
it, for with the inhibition of aging has come, as well,
unbelievable good health. That was something that
had worried us to start with—with all the people
gone, what would we do for doctors or hospital care
if we should happen to fall ill? Luckily, perhaps,
the chronological years during which a woman remains capable of bearing children are about the same
as they were before the span of life was lengthened.
The female reproductive system apparently exhausts
its supply of potential egg cells within some thirty
years or so, as it did before.

There can be little doubt that the disappearance
of the human race and the inhibiting of aging must
somehow be connected. And while none of us can
help but be grateful for this longer life and, perhaps
as well, for the lifting of the social pressure which
came with the overpopulation of the planet, the more
thoughtful of us sometimes worry about the implications which may lie behind it all. In the dark of
night we lie unsleeping in our beds and think of it
and although the shock has faded with the years, we
are sometimes frightened.

So on this August morning near the end of the
twenty-second century since the birth of Jesus, I begin this record in which I shall set down, in detail,
my remembrance of what has happened. It is a job
that someone should do and, as the oldest member
of this house, in my hundred and tenth chronological
year, it seems only mete and proper that mine should
be the hand to put down the words. Without a record
of this sort, inscribed while human memory serves
with some faithfulness, what happened to the race
would become, in time, a myth . . .

2

He could not forget that last bear but, strangely, could not remember exactly what had happened. Trying to remember, trying to be sure, had occupied his thoughts for the last few days and he was no nearer to an answer than he had ever been. The beast, rearing up from a deep-cut stream bed, had caught him off his guard and there had been no chance to run, for the bear was far too close. The arrow had not killed it, he was sure of that, for there was little time to shoot and the shaft had been badly placed. Yet the bear had died, lunging forward to skid almost to his feet. And in that fractured moment before the bear had died, something had happened and it was this something that had happened that he could not remember. It was, he was certain, something he had done, but there was no clue to what it might have been. There had been times when the answer had welled almost to awareness and then been driven back, deep into his mind, as if it were something he was not supposed to know, or that he would be better off not knowing, something that his inner, hidden mind would not let him know.

He dropped his pack beside him and leaned the bow against it. Staring out across the wide expanse of bluff-rimmed, autumn-painted valley where the two great rivers met, he saw that it was exactly as he had been told it would be by the buffalo-hunting band he'd met in the great high plains almost a moon before. He smiled to himself as he thought of them, for they had been pleasant people. They had asked him to stay and he very nearly had. There had been a girl who had laughed with him, the laughter deep inside her throat, and a young man who had laid his hand upon his arm with the touch of brotherhood. But in the end he could not stay.

The sun was coming up and the maples along the rim of the farther bluff, caught in its rays, flamed with sudden red and gold. And there, on the rocky headland that reared above the river's junction, stood the huge block of masonry that they had told him of, with its many chimneys pointing stubby fingers at the sky.

The young man lifted a pair of binoculars off his chest and set them to his eyes. Disturbed by the movement of the strap, the bear claws of his necklace clicked together.

Jason Whitney came to the end of his morning walk and it had been, he told himself, the best walk he'd ever had—although he recalled that he always thought that each morning as he came up the slight slope toward the patio, with the smell of frying bacon and of morning eggs wafting from the kitchen, where Thatcher made them ready. But this morning had been good, he insisted to himself. It had been so fresh, with just a nip of chill until the rising sun dispelled it, and the leaves, he thought—the leaves were at their best. He had stood out on the point of rocks and had watched the rivers and they had been (perhaps to complement the autumn colors through which they flowed) a deeper blue than usual. A flock of ducks had been flying across the bottom land, close above the treetops, and in one of the little ponds which dotted the flood plain a moose had stood knee-deep, putting his head down into the water to feed upon the lilies, the water cascading off his mighty antlers when he raised his head. Even from where he stood, Jason had imagined he could hear that sound of cascading water, although he knew it was too far to hear.

The two dogs that had gone with him had hurried on ahead and now were waiting on the patio, not for him, although he would have liked to think so, but for their plates of food. Bowser, full of many years, had walked heavily and sedately beside him as they'd gone down across the land, while Rover, the foolish pup, had treed an early-foraging squirrel in the walnut grove and had flushed a covey of quail out of the corn shocks and pumpkins of an autumn field.

The door opened on the patio and Martha came out, carrying plates for the two dogs. She stooped and set them on the stones, while the dogs waited, respectfully and politely, with their tails swinging slowly and their ears pricked forward. Straightening, she came off the patio and down the slope to meet him. She gave him her morning kiss and linked her arm in his.

"While you were on your walk," she said, "I had a talk with Nancy."

He knitted his brow, trying to remember. "Nancy?" he asked.

"Why, of course," she said. "You know. She is Geoffrey's oldest child. It has been so long since I have talked with her."

He knitted his brow, trying to remember. "Nancy?" he asked.

"Out Polaris way," said Martha. "They moved just recently. They're on the nicest planet . . ."

*   *   *

Evening Star, crouched in the lodge, put the finishing touches to the talismanic doll. She had worked hard on it to make it nice and this was the day she'd take it as an offering to the oak. It was a good day for it, she told herself—fair and soft and warm. These were the kind of days that one must treasure, close against the heart, for the painted days were few. Soon would come the dreary days, with the cold mist slanting ghostily through the naked trees and after that the frigid sweep of northern winds and snow. Outside she heard the camp come to morning life—the ring of ax on wood, the clatter of the cooking pots, the call of friend to friend, the happy barking of a dog. Later in the day the work of clearing the old fields would take up again, grubbing out the brush, clearing away the stones heaved up by the frosts of other years, the raking and burning of the weeds, leaving the ground bare and ready for the springtime plowing and the planting. Everyone would be busy (as she herself would be expected to be) and it would be easy for her to leave the camp unnoticed and to get back again before anyone should remark her absence.

She must let no one know, she reminded herself—not her father or mother and least of all Red Cloud, the first chieftain of the band and her own grandfather, many times removed. For it was not proper that a woman should have a guardian spirit. Except that to her it seemed entirely right. On that day seven years ago the signs of guardianship had been too plain to doubt. The tree had spoken to her and she had spoken to the tree and it was as if a father and a daughter had bespoken one another. It was not, she thought, as if she had sought the relationship. It had been the last thing in her mind. But when a tree speaks to one, what is one to do?

On this day, she wondered, would the tree speak

to her again? After so long an absence, would this tree remember?

Hezekiah sat on the marble bench beneath the drooping branches of the ancient willow tree and pulled the coarse brown robe close about his metal frame—and this was pretense and pride, he thought, and unworthy of him, for he did not need to sit and he did not need the robe. A yellow leaf fluttered down from overhead and settled in his lap, a clear, almost transparent yellow against the brownness of the robe. He moved to brush it off and then he let it stay. For who am I, he thought, to interfere with or dispute even such a simple thing as the falling of a leaf.

He lifted his eyes from the leaf and over there, a mile or so away, beyond the monastery walls, the great house of stone stood solid on the rocky battlement that rose above the rivers—a mighty, sprawling house with its windows winking in the morning sun, the chimney's pleading hands lifted up to God.

They are the ones who should be here instead of us, he thought, the people in that house, and then, almost as soon as he thought of it, recalled that for many centuries there had been only two of them in residence, Jason Whitney and his good wife, Martha. At times some of the others came back from the stars to visit their old home or the old family home (whichever it might be, for some of them had been born far among the stars). And what business did they have, Hezekiah asked, with a touch of bitterness, to be out among the stars? Their concern should not be with the stars and all that they might find to amuse themselves out there; any human's one concern rightfully should be the condition of his immortal soul.

In the grove of music trees beyond the monastery

walls the leaves were rustling gently, but as yet the trees were silent. Later in the day, sometime in the afternoon, they'd do some tuning up for the nightly concert. It would be, he thought, with some reluctance at the thought, a glorious thing to hear. At times he had imagined their music was that of some heavenly choir, but it was all, he knew, in his imagination; at times the kind of music they produced was anything but churchly. It was thoughts like this, he told himself, and the action of sitting on a bench and the wearing of a robe that made himself and his companions less fit to perform with faith the task they'd taken up. But a naked robot, he told himself, could not stand before the Lord; he must have about him some of the habiliments of man if he were to take the place of man, who had so utterly forgotten.

The doubts and fears came flooding into him and he sat bowed against them. It would seem, he thought, one would become accustomed to them, for they'd been with him from the start (and with the others, too), but the sharpness of them had not dulled and they still cut him to the core. Rather than diminishing with familiarity, they had grown sharper as the years went on, with no answer found after centuries of poring over the meticulous commentaries and the extensive, searching writings of the human theologians. Was all of this, he asked himself in anguish, no more than a monstrous blasphemy? Could entities that had no souls minister to the Lord? Or might they, in their years of faith and work, have developed souls? He searched for a soul deep inside himself (and it was not the first time he had searched) and could find no soul. Even if there were one, he wondered, how could it be recognized? What ingredients went into the formation of a soul? Could one, in fact, be fashioned or need one be born with it—and if that should be the case, what genetic patterns were involved?

Were he and his fellow robots (his fellow monks?)

usurping human rights? Were they, in sinful pride, aspiring to something reserved for the human race? Was it—had it ever been—within their province to attempt to maintain a human and a Godly institution that the humans had rejected and which even now God might not care about?

3

After breakfast, in the hushed quiet of the library, Jason Whitney sat at his desk and opened one of the bound record books which he had picked from a long row of its fellows on the shelf behind him. He saw that it had been more than a month since he had made an entry. Not, he thought, that there had been any real reason to make an entry then. Life ran so placidly that there were few ripples to record. Perhaps it would be better to put the book back on the shelf with nothing written in it, although it seemed, somehow, an act of faith to write an occasional paragraph at not too long an interval from the last one written. In the last month nothing of any consequence had happened—no one had come back to visit, there had been nothing but routine contacts from those out among the stars, there had been no word of the Indian bands, there had been no robots passing by and stopping, so there had been no news—although what the robots brought was rumor more often than it was news. There had been gossip, of course. Martha kept up a running conversation with others of the clan and when they sat on the patio to hear the nightly concert, she would fill him in on what had been said that day. But mostly it was woman talk and nothing to put down.

A narrow shaft of morning sun, slotted through the slit where the heavy drapes at one of the tall windows failed to come together, fell across him, lighting up the gray hair and the square and solid shoulders. He was a tall man, thin, but with a sense of strength that offset the thinness. His face was rugged, creased with tiny lines. The mustache bristled and was matched by the craggy brows that sat above the deep-sunken eyes that held a steely look in them. He sat in the chair, unmoving, looking at the room and wondering again at the quiet satisfaction that he always found within it, and at times more than satisfaction, as if the room, with its book-lined loftiness and vastness, carried a special benediction. The thoughts of many men, he told himself, resided in this space—all the great thinkers of the world held secure between the bindings of the volumes on the shelves, selected and placed there long ago by his grandfather so that in the days to come the essence of the human race, the heritage of recorded thought, would always be at hand. He recalled that he had often held the conceit that the essential characters of these ancient writers, the ghostly presence of the men themselves, had in the passing years settled on this room and late at night, when all else was quiet, he had often found himself conversing with these olden men, who emerged from the dust of the past into the shadow of the present.

The tier of books ran all around the room, broken only by two doors and, on the river side, three windows. When the first tier ended a balcony began, guarded by decorative metal railing, and on the balcony the second tier of books went all around the room. Above one of the doors a clock was mounted on the wall and for more than five thousand years, he reminded himself in wonder, the clock had kept on ticking, beating off the seconds century on century. The clock said 9:15 and how near, he wondered, was that to the correctness of the time as set up by men so many years ago. There was, he realized, no way that one might know, although it did not matter now. The world would be as well off if there were no clock.

Muffled sounds made their way into the room—the mournful lowing of a distant cow, the nearby barking of a dog, the insane cackling of a hen. The music trees still were silent—they'd not start tuning up until sometime in the afternoon. He wondered if they'd try one of the new compositions tonight. There had, of late, been a lot of them. If so, he hoped it would not be one of the experimental ones they had been trying lately. There were so many others they might play, so many of the old and favorite ones, but there was no sense to what they did. It seemed, he told himself, that it had been getting worse in the last few years since two of the older trees had shown some sign of dying. They had begun to lose some of their branches and each spring it seemed that their leaf output was smaller. There were young saplings to take their place, of course, and that might be the trouble. He put up his hand and brushed a finger across his mustache, worriedly. He wished for the thousandth time that he knew something about the care of trees. He had looked through some of the books, of course, but there seemed nothing there that would be of any help. And even if there were, one could not be sure that the music trees would respond to the treatment as would a tree of Earth.

At the sound of padding feet, he turned. The robot, Thatcher, was coming through the door.

"Yes, what is it, Thatcher?"

"It is Mr. Horace Red Cloud, sir."

"But Horace is up north. In the wild rice country."

"It seems, sir, the band has moved. They are camped down by the river, in their old camping grounds. They plan to restore the old fields and put in a crop next spring."

"You had a talk with him?"

"Sir," said Thatcher, "he is an old acquaintance and, naturally, I passed a few words with him. He brought a bag of rice."

"I hope you thanked him, Thatcher."

"Oh, indeed I did, sir."

"You should have brought him in."

"He said he had no desire to disturb you, sir, if you happened to be busy."

"I am never really busy. Surely you know that."

"Then," said Thatcher, "I'll ask him to step in."

Jason rose and walked around the desk, standing beside it, waiting for his friend. How long had it been, he wondered—four years, or five—it surely must be five. He'd gone down to the camp to bid his old friend good-bye and after the band had embarked, had stood for a long time on the shingle of the shore, watching the long line of canoes move swiftly up the river, paddles flashing in the sunlight.

Red Cloud was the same age as Jason, but had a younger look. When he came into the room and across the carpeting, his stride had a young man's spring. His hair was black, without a trace of gray; it was parted exactly down the center of his scalp and hung in two heavy braids across his shoulders to dangle on his chest. His face was weather-beaten but, except for a tiny network of crow's feet at the corner of his eyes, had not a wrinkle in it. He wore a buckskin shirt and leggings, with moccasins on his feet. The hand he held out to Jason was thick and calloused with short, blunt fingers.

"It has been a long time, Horace," Jason said. "I am glad to see you."

"You are the only one," said Red Cloud, "who still calls me Horace."

"All right, then," said Jason, "shall I call you Chief? Or Cloud? Or maybe Red?"

Red Cloud grinned. "From you, Jason, Horace sounds just fine. We were boys together. Surely you remember. And it brings back the times when we roamed the woods together. We nicked our wrists and held the cuts together so that our blood would mingle. Or at least we thought that it would mingle. I rather doubt it did. But that is neither here nor there. The important thing was the symbolism."

"I remember," Jason said. "I can remember that first day, when your band came paddling down the river and saw the smoke rising from one of our chimneys. All of you, the whole kit and caboodle of you, came swarming up the hill to see what it was all about and for the first time both your band and the people at this house learned that they were not alone, but there still were others left."

"We built big fires out on the lawn," said Red Cloud, "and we killed a beef or two and had a barbecue. We joined hands in a ring and danced around the fires, whooping and hollering. Your grandfather of blessed memory rolled out a keg of whiskey and we all got rather drunk."

"That was when you and I first met," said Jason. "Two young sprouts out to show the world—except there was no world to show. We took to one another almost immediately. We went hunting and fishing together and we roamed the hills. And we chased the girls."

"We caught some of them, as I recall," said Red Cloud.

"They weren't hard to catch," said Jason.

They stood, looking into one another's face, silently, then Jason said, "Let's sit down. There must be a lot we need to talk about."

Red Cloud sat down in a chair and Jason took another and spun it around so he could face his friend.

"How long has it been?" he asked.

"Six years."

"You just arrived?"

"A week ago," said Red Cloud. "We left the north after the wild rice harvest. We didn't travel fast. We stopped whenever we found a good camping place and loafed around and hunted. Some of our young men took the horses down west of the river and will hold them there until there is ice to cross. Later, when it gets colder, we'll cross over and hunt for winter meat. Buffalo and wild cattle. A runner came in last night and said there are a lot of them on the prairies."

Jason frowned. "A week, you say. You shouldn't have waited so long. If you didn't have time yourself, you should have sent a runner. I'd have come down to visit you."

"The time went fast. There was much to do. We are trying to get the corn ground into shape. The fields have grown up to brush and weeds. We ran out of corn and got hungry for it. Tried to grow some up north, but the season was too short. Got it in late and the frost caught it. Had some roasting ears, but that was all."

"We have corn," said Jason. "A lot of it, ground and ready. I'll send some down to the camp before the day is over. What else do you need—bacon, eggs, flour? We have some good wheat flour. More by far than we can use. Cloth, if you want it. The wool has been good and the looms busy."

"Jason, I didn't come begging . . ."

"I know you didn't. For years we've shared things back and forth. I hate to think of how much meat and fish and berries and other things your folks packed up the hill for us in days gone by. Thatcher says you brought some rice . . ."

"All right," said Red Cloud. "You'll not object to a supply of buffalo meat when we make the hunt?"

"Not at all," said Jason.

"Better yet, how about coming along on the hunt?"

"There is nothing I'd like better."

"Good! It will be like old times. We'll let the others do the work. We'll sit around the fire, you and I, and talk and eat hump meat."

"You live a good life, Horace."

"I think we do. There were so many ways we could have gone. We could have settled down. We could have taken over some good housing and good fields and put in crops and collected us some livestock. We could have become good farmers. But we didn't. We took up the old ways. I guess we never were too far from them. In the heart of each of us, we'd dreamed of them time and yet again. The pull was there. The call was there. Our ancestors had lived the life for thousands of years. We had only a few hundred years of the white man's way and they had been far from good years. We never fitted in, we never had a chance to. It was a relief to shuck off all of it and go back to the flowers, the trees, the clouds, the seasons and the weather, the running water, the creatures of the woods and prairies—to make them a part of us again, more a part of us than they'd ever been before. We learned something from the whites, that we can't deny—we'd have been stupid if we hadn't. And we used these white man's ways to make the old way of life an even better life. Sometimes I wonder if we made the right choice, then I see an autumn leaf—one leaf alone, not a lot of leaves—or hear the sound of a little stream of water running in the woods, or catch a forest scent, and then I know we were not wrong. We went back to the earth, linked ourselves with the hills and streams, and that is the way it should be. That is the way we were meant to live. Not back to the old tribal concept, but back to a way of life. We were a woodland tribe to start with, but now we are no longer woodland. Maybe we're simply Indian. We adopted the skin tepee of the Western plains tribes and, in large part, their way of dress and their use of horses. But we kept the birch bark canoe, the wild rice harvest and the maple sugar. It has been a good life. You and I, old friend, have caught the feel of life—I in my tepee, you in this stone house. You never went to the stars and you may be better off for never having gone. I suppose they find great things out there . . ."

"A few things," Jason said. "Many interesting things. Perhaps even some useful items. But we put few of them to any use. We have seen them, observed them, even studied them, in some cases arrived at an understanding of what is going on. But we no longer are a technological race. We lost technology when we lost the manpower and the knowledge and the machines broke down and there was no one to start them up again and no energy to run them. We don't mourn that lost technology, as I think you know. At one time we might have, but not any longer. It would be a bother now. We have become competent observers and we gain our satisfaction from our observations, achieving minor triumphs when we are able to reach some solid understanding. Knowing is the goal, not the using. We aren't users. We have somehow risen above using. We can rest content to see resources lying idle; we might even think it shameful to try to use or harness them. And it's not only resources; it's ideas and . . ."

"How much do you remember, Jason? How much, really, from the old days? Not how our tribe found your people, but all the rest of it."

"I remember rather vividly," said Jason. "And so should you. You were a young man, with me, when it happened. We were both at the impressionable age. It should have made a great impact on us."

Red Cloud shook his head. "My memory is dim. There are too many other things. I can scarcely remember any other life than the one we live today."

"My remembrance is in a book, or in many books," said Jason, gesturing at the shelf behind the desk. "It all is written down. My grandfather began it, some fifty years after it happened, writing it down so we'd not forget, so it would not become a myth. He wrote all that he could remember of what had happened and once that was finished, he made regular entries. When he finally died, I took up the work. It all is written down, from the day it happened."

"And when you die," asked Red Cloud, "who then will do the writing?"

"I do not know," said Jason.

"Jason, a thing I have often wondered, but have never asked. May I ask it now?"

"Certainly. Anything at all."

"Why did you never go out to the stars?"

"Perhaps because I can't."

"But you never tried. You never really wanted to."

"The others went out one by one," said Jason, "until only Martha and I were left. It seemed that someone should stay. It seemed that we should not leave Earth entirely. Someone belonged here. An anchor man, perhaps, for the others who had gone. To keep the home fires burning. Be here to welcome the others back when they wanted to come home. To keep a place for them."

"They do come back, of course. And you are here to welcome them."

"Some of them," said Jason. "Not all. My brother, John, was one of the first to go. He has not been back. We've had no word of him. I often wonder where he is. If he is still alive."

"You imply a responsibility to stay. But, Jason, that can't be the entire story."

"It's part of it, I think. At one time more a part of it than it is now. John and I were the oldest. My sister, Janice, is younger. We still see her occasionally and Martha talks with her quite often. If John had stayed, Martha and I might have gone. I said maybe we didn't because we couldn't. I don't really believe that. The ability seems to be inherent. Man probably had it for a long time before he began to use it. For it to develop time was needed and the longer life gave us time. Perhaps it would have developed even without the longer life if we'd not been so concerned, so fouled up, with our technology. Somewhere we may have taken the wrong turning, accepted the wrong values and permitted our concern with technology to mask our real and valid purpose. The concern with technology may have kept us from knowing what we had. These abilities of ours could not struggle up into our consciousness through the thick layers of machines and cost estimates and all the rest of it. And when we talk about abilities, it's not simply going to the stars. Your people don't go to the stars. There may be no need of you to do so. You have become, instead, a part of your environment, living within its texture and understanding it. It went that way for you . . ."

"But if you could go, why don't you? Surely you could be away for a little time. The robots would take care of things. They'd keep the home fires burning, keep the welcome ready for those who wanted to return."

Jason shook his head. "It is too late now. I fall increasingly in love with this house and with these acres as the years go on. I feel a part of it. I'd be lost without the house and land—and Earth. I couldn't live without them. A man can't walk the same land, live in the same house, for almost five thousand years . . ."

"I know," said Red Cloud. "The band, as its members increased, split up and scattered, becoming many bands. Some are on the prairies, others eastward in the forests. I stick to these two rivers . . ."

"I am guilty of bad manners," Jason said. "I should have asked first off. How is Mrs. Cloud?"

"Happy. With a new camp to boss, she is in her glory."

"And your sons and grandsons many times removed?"

"Only a few of the grandsons still are with us," Red Cloud said. "The sons and other grandsons are with other bands. We hear from them at times. Running Elk, my grandson thrice removed, was killed by a grizzly about a year ago. A runner came to tell us. Otherwise they all are well and happy."

"I grieve for you," said Jason. "Running Elk was a grandson to be proud of."

Red Cloud bowed his head in thanks. "Mrs. Jason, I gather, is in good health."

Jason nodded. "She spends a lot of time talking with the others. She is most proficient at it. Much more so than I am. Telepathy seems to be second nature to her. Each evening she has much news to tell. There are a lot of us now. I have no idea how many. Martha would know better than I do. She keeps it all in mind. All the relationships, who married whom and so on. Some thousands of us, surely."

"You told me once before, many years ago, that some intelligences had been found in space, but none like us. In the years since we've been gone . . ."

"You're right," said Jason. "None like us. Some contacts. Some friendly, some not so friendly, some indifferent to us. The most of them so alien to us they set one's teeth on edge. And, of course, the wandering alien travelers that sometimes visit Earth."

"And that is all? No cooperating . . ."

"No, that isn't all," said Jason. "Something has arisen that is most disturbing. A whiff of something most disturbing. Like a bad smell on the wind. From somewhere out in the center . . ."

"The center of what, Jason?"

"The center of the galaxy. The core. An intelligence of some sort. We just sniffed the edge of it and that's enough . . ."

"Hostile?"

"No, not hostile. Cold. Intelligent, too intelligent.

Cold and indifferent. Analytical. Oh, hell, I can't tell you. There's no way to tell you. As if an angleworm could sniff the intelligence of a human. More than that. More difference between it and us than there is between man and angleworm."

"It's got you scared?"

"Scared? I guess so. Upset. Apprehensive. Only comfort is that we probably are beneath their notice."

"Then why worry?"

"Not worrying too much. It isn't that. Just that a man feels uncertain knowing there is something like that in the galaxy with him. As if you stumbled across a pit of concentrated evil."

"But it isn't evil."

"I don't think so. I don't know what it is. Neither does anyone else. We just caught a whiff . . ."

"You haven't detected it? You, yourself?"

"No. Some of the others. Two of the others out in the stars."

"No need to worry, more than likely. Just stay out of the way. I wonder, though—could it have had something to do with the People leaving? It seems unlikely, though. You still have no idea, Jason, of why it happened, why all the People went away."

"None at all," said Jason.

"You were speaking of the aliens that came to Earth . . ."

"Yes," said Jason. "It is strange how they come to Earth these days. Not many of them, of course. Not many that we know about. Two or three in the last century, although I guess, when you come to think of it, with all the space there is and the distances, that is quite a lot. But they never seemed to come before. It's only happened since the People left. Although it is possible they may have been coming in the old days and were never seen, or if seen, unrecognized for what they were. Maybe we didn't see them because we were unprepared to recognize them. Even if we'd seen them, we would have closed our eyes to them. We'd have felt uncomfortable in the presence of something that we couldn't understand and so, with one grand gesture, we'd have wiped them all away. We would have said they can't be here, they aren't here, we never saw them, and that would be the end of it."

"That may have been it," said Red Cloud. "Or far fewer may have come. We were a turbulent planet, seething with intelligence and at times a rather terrifying kind of intelligence. On a smaller scale, maybe something like that intelligence of yours in the center of the galaxy. Surely not the sort of place a wandering alien would have chosen to sit down to seek a time of rest. For he would have had no rest. In those days there was no rest for anyone."

"You are right, of course," said Jason. "We know it now. I don't suppose there was any way we could have known it then. We got ahead. We progressed . . ."

"You have talked, I think," said Red Cloud, "with some of the wandering aliens."

"Two or three of them. Once I traveled five hundred miles to talk with one of them, but it was gone by the time I got there. A robot brought the news. I'm not as good as Martha with this business of galactic telepathy, but I can talk with aliens. With some of them, that is. I seem to have the knack for it. Sometimes, though, there is no way of talking. They have no basis for recognizing sound waves as a means of communication and a human, on his part, may not even have the sense to recognize the signals or the mental waves they use for communication. With others of them, even if the means of communication is there, you can't do any talking. There's really nothing to talk about. No common grounds for talking."

"This matter of wandering aliens," said Red Cloud, "is partly why I came. I'd have come anyhow, of course, the first day that I could. But I wanted to tell you that we have an alien here. Up at the head of Cat Den Hollow. Little Wolf found him and came running and I went to have a look."

So this was it, thought Jason; he should have known. All this careful, polite talking on everything except the one thing that Red Cloud had really come to tell him, and finally it was out. It was the way they were; one should expect it of them. The old unhurried way, the tribal protocol, the dignity. To never be excited, to not come charging in, to be leisurely and deliberate and to make ground for decency.

"You tried to talk with him?" he asked.

"No," said Horace Red Cloud. "I can talk with flowers and flowing rivers and they can talk back to me, but an alien—I'd not know how to start."

"All right," said Jason, "I'll amble over and see what it has in mind, if it has anything in mind. That is, if I can talk with it. Was there any indication of how it might have come?"

"It's a teleporter, I would guess. There was no sign of any kind of ship."

"Usually they are," said Jason. "The same as us. A machine of any sort is a cumbersome contraption. Star-roving is nothing new, of course, although at first we thought it was. We thought we had made such a wonderful discovery when the first of us began to develop and employ parapsychic powers. But it was not so wonderful; it was simply something that we'd been too busy, as a technological race, to take the time to look at. And even if someone had thought about it and had tried to talk about it, he would have been ridiculed."

"None of us have star-roved," Red Cloud said. "I'm not sure any of us have any powers at all. We have been so occupied with the world we live in and the secrets that it holds that we may not have tapped the secret resources that we have, if there should be any. But now . . ."

"I think you have powers and are using them," Jason told him, "to the best of purposes. You know your environment and mesh more closely with it than men ever have before. This must take some sort of psychic instinct. It may not be as romantic as star-roving, but it takes, perhaps, an even greater understanding."

"I thank you for your kindness," Red Cloud said, "and there may be certain truth in what you say. I have a beautiful and very foolish granddaughter-many-times-removed who has only turned her nineteenth year. Perhaps you remember her—the Evening Star."

"Why, of course I do," Jason said, delighted. "When you were away from camp or busy and I came visiting, she would take me over. We went on nature hikes and she showed me birds and flowers and other woodland wonders, and she chattered all the time, most delightfully."

"She still chatters most delightfully, but I am somewhat concerned by her. I think, perhaps, she has some of the brand of psychic power that your clan may hold . . ."

"You mean star-roving?"

Red Cloud crinkled up his face. "I'm not sure. No, I don't think so. It may be something else. I sense a certain strangeness in her. I suppose I am disturbed by it, although I have no right to be. She has a thirst for knowledge such as I have never seen in any of my people. Not a thirst to know her world, although that is there as well, but a thirst to know outside her world. To know all that's ever happened, all that men have thought. She has read all the books that the band possesses and they are very few . . ."

Jason raised his arm and swept it in an arc to indicate the room. "There are books here," he said, "if she would come and read them. Down in the basement areas there are other rooms stacked to the ceilings with others of them. She is free to use any that she wishes, but I am reluctant to let any leave this house. Once lost, a book would be irreplaceable."

"I had come prepared to ask," said Red Cloud. "I was leading up to it. Thank you for offering."

"It pleases me there is someone who might wish to read them. It is a privilege to share them with her, I assure you."

"I suppose," said Red Cloud, "we should have given thought to books, but it's a little late now to do anything about it. There might still be books, of course, although time, I would imagine, has destroyed most of them. Weather and the rodents would have gotten at them. And our people hesitate to go looking for them. We have a great dislike for the ancient places. They are so old and musty and are filled with many ghosts—ghosts of the past that even now we do not like to think about. We have a few books, of course, and treasure them as an ancient heritage. And we make it a point of honor with the past each child is taught to read. But for most of them it is an unpleasant duty only. Until the Evening Star, there have been few who cared to read."

"Would Evening Star," asked Jason, "be willing to come and live with us? For as long as she might like. It would brighten up the house to have a youngster in it and I would undertake to guide her in her reading."

"I shall tell her," Red Cloud said. "She will be delighted. You know, of course, she calls you Uncle Jason."

"No, I did not know," said Jason. "I am honored."

Silence fell upon the two men and they sat there for a moment in the hush of the library. Upon the wall the clock ticked off the seconds, loudly in the silence.

Red Cloud stirred. "Jason, you have kept track of time. Of the years, I mean. You even have a clock. We have no clocks and we've kept no count.

We didn't bother to. We took each day as it came and lived it to the full. We live not with days, but seasons. And we have not counted seasons."

"Here and there," said Jason, "we may have missed a day or two, or added a day or two—I can't be sure of that. But we have kept count. It's been five thousand years. I'm as old, physically, as my grandfather was when he first wrote in the books. After that he lived for almost three thousand years. If I follow the same schedule, I'll live a full eight thousand years. It does not seem possible, of course. It seems a bit indecent for a man to live eight thousand years."

"Some day," said Red Cloud, "we may know what brought about all this—where the People went to and why we live so long."

"Perhaps," said Jason, "although I have no hope. I have been thinking, Horace . . ."

"Yes?"

"I could round up a gang of robots and send them down to clear those cornfields for you. They're just messing around, not doing much of anything. I know how you feel about robots, of course . . ."

"No. Thank you very much. We'll accept the corn and flour and all the rest of it, but we can't accept the help of robots."

"What, actually, have you got against them? Don't you trust them? They won't hang around. They won't bother you. They'll just clear the fields, then leave."

"We feel uneasy with them," Red Cloud said. "They don't fit in with us. They're a reminder of what happened to us when the white men came. When we broke, we broke completely. We kept only a few things. The simple metal tools, the plow, a better economic sense—we no longer feast one day and starve the next as the Indians did in many instances before the white men came. We went back to the old woods life, the old plains life. We went on our own; we have to keep it that way."

"I think I understand."

"I'm not entirely sure we trust them, either," Red Cloud said. "Not completely. Maybe the ones you have here, working in your fields for you and doing other things, may be all right. But I have my reservations about some of the wild ones. I told you, didn't I, that there is a gang of them up the river, at the site of some old city . . ."

"Yes, I remember that you did. Minneapolis and St. Paul. You saw them many, many years ago. They were building something."

"They still are building it," said Red Cloud. "We stopped on the way downstream and had a look—a far-off look. There are more of them than ever and they still are building. One great building, although it doesn't look like a building. The robots wouldn't be building a house, would they?"

"I don't think so. Not for themselves. They laugh at weather. They're made of some sort of almost indestructible alloy. It doesn't rust, it doesn't wear, it resists almost everything. Weather, temperature, rain . . . none of them mean a thing to them."

"We didn't hang around too long," said Red Cloud. "We stayed a good ways off. We used glasses, but still couldn't see too much. We were scared, I guess. Uncomfortable. We got out of there once we had a look. I don't suppose there is any real danger, but we took no chances."

4

Evening Star walked through the morning and talked with the friends she met. Be careful, rabbit, nibbling at your clover; a red fox has his den just across the hill. And why do you chatter, little bushy-tail, and stamp your feet at me: it is your friend who is walking past. You took all the hickory nuts from the three big trees at the hollow's mouth before I could get to them and have them stored away. You should be happy, for you're the most fortunate of squirrels. You have a deep den in a hollow oak where you'll be snug and happy when the winter comes and you have food hidden everywhere. Chickadee, you are out of place and time, swinging on the thistle stalk. You should not be here so soon. You come only when there are snowflakes in the air. Did you steal a march upon your fellows; you'll be lonesome here until the others come. Or are you like myself, cherishing the last few golden days before the chill moves down?

She walked through the sun of morning, with the colored pageant of the open woods burst into flame and gold about her. She saw the burnished metal of the goldenrod, the sky-blue of the asters. She walked upon the grass that once had been lush and green and now was turning tawny and was slippery beneath her moccasins. She knelt to brush her hand against the green and scarlet carpet of the lichen patches growing on an old, gray boulder and she sang within herself because she was a part of it—yes, even of the lichens, even of the boulder.

She came to the top of the ridge that she was climbing and below her lay the denser forest that cloaked the river hills. A hollow dipped down between the slopes rising on each side and she followed it. A spring flowed out of a limestone outcrop and she went on down the hollow, walking to the music of hidden, singing water flowing from the spring. Her memory winged back to that other day. It had been summer then, with the hills a froth of green and birds still singing in the trees. She clasped the doll she carried close against her breast and again she heard the words the tree had spoken to her. It all was wrong, of course, for no woman should make a compact with a thing so strong and lordly as a tree. A birch, perhaps, or a poplar, or one of the lesser, more feminine of trees—that, while it would be frowned upon still might be understandable. But the tree that had spoken to her had been an ancient white oak—a hunter's tree.

It stood just ahead of her, old and gnarled and strong, but despite all its girth and strength seeming to crouch against the ground, as if it were a thing embattled. Its leaves were brown and had begun to wither, but it had not lost them yet. It still clung to its warrior's cloak while some of the other trees nearby stood in nakedness.

She clambered down to reach it and, having reached it, found the rotted, flaking hollow that gouged into its massive trunk. Standing on tiptoe, she saw that the secret hollow place still held and guarded the doll she'd placed there all those years before—a little corncob doll dressed in scraps of woolen cloth. It had weathered and been darkened by the rain that had seeped into the hollow and

soaked it time and time again, but it held its shape,
it still clung against the tree.

Still standing on tiptoe, she placed the doll she
carried into the hollow, settling it carefully beside
the first doll. Then she stepped away.

"Old Grandfather," she said, her eyes looking at
the ground as a matter of respect, "I went away, but
I did not forget you. In the long nights and the bright
noons I remembered you. Now I have come back
again to tell you that I may go away again, although
in a different way. But I'll never leave completely,
because I love this world too much. And I shall
always reach out to you, knowing you will know
when I hold out my arms and I shall know that upon
this land stands one I can believe and depend upon.
I am truly grateful to you, Old Grandfather, for the
strength you give me and for your understanding."

She stopped and waited for an answer and there
was no answer. The tree did not talk to her as it
had that first time.

"I do not know where I'll be going," she told the
tree, "or when I'll go or even if I'll go at all, but I
came to tell you. To share with you a feeling I can
share with no one else."

She waited once again for the tree to answer and
there were no words, but it seemed to her that the
great oak stirred, as if arousing from a sleep, and
she had the sense of great arms lifted and held above
her head and there was something—benediction?—
that came out from the tree and settled over her.

She backed away slowly, step by step, her eyes
still upon the ground, then she turned and fled, running wildly up the hill, filled with that sense of
something that had come forth from the tree and
touched her.

She tripped on a surface root that looped out of
the forest floor, caught herself against a huge fallen
tree trunk, and sat down on it. Looking back, she

saw that the ancient oak was no longer in sight.
There were too many intervening trees.

The woods were quiet. Nothing stirred in the un-
derbrush and there were no birds. In the spring and
summer this place was filled with birds, but now
there was none. They either had gone south or were
elsewhere, flocking up, ready for the move. Down
in the river bottoms vast flocks of ducks quarreled
and chortled in the sloughs and the reed patches were
filled with great flocks of blackbirds that went storm-
ing up into the sky like hurtling sleet. But here the
gentler birds were gone and the woods were quiet,
a solemn quietness that held a touch of loneliness.

She had told the tree that she might be going
elsewhere and she wondered if she had said what she
really meant or if she knew as much as she should
know about this going elsewhere. It sometimes
seemed that she might be going to another place—
and it might not be that at all. There was in her a
feeling of unease, of expectation, the prickling sensa-
tion that something most momentous was about to
happen, but she could not define it. It was an un-
familiar thing, a rather frightening thing to someone
who had lived all her life in a world she knew so
intimately. The world was full of friends—not only
human friends, but many other friends, the little scur-
riers of the woods and brush, the shy flowers hidden
in their woodland nooks, the graceful trees that stood
against the sky, the very wind and weather.

She patted the old decaying trunk as if it might be
a friend as well and saw how the briars and high-
growing forest plants had gathered all around it,
rallying to its defense, hiding it in its hour of indig-
nity and need.

She rose from the trunk and went on up the hill,
going slowly now, no longer running. She had left
the doll and the tree had not spoken as it had before,
but it had done something else, performed some
other act and everything was well.

She reached the crest of the steep river slope and started down the reverse side, heading for the camp, and as she started to angle down the hill realized, suddenly, without actually seeing, that she was not alone. She turned swiftly and there he stood, clad only in a breech clout, his bronzed body smooth and hard and shining in the sun, his pack beside him and the bow leaned against the pack. A pair of binoculars hung from their strap about his neck, half hiding the necklace that he wore.

"Do I intrude upon your land?" he asked, politely.

"The land is free," she said.

She was fascinated by the necklace. She kept staring at it.

He touched it with his finger. "Vanity," he said.

"You killed the great white bear," she said. "More than one, from all the claws there are."

"Also," he said, "a way to keep the count. One claw, one bear. A claw from each."

She drew in her breath. "Your medicine is strong."

He slapped the bow. "My bow is strong. My arrows true and tipped with flint. Flint is better than anything except the finest steel and where now do you find the finest steel."

"You came from the West," she said. She knew that the great white bears lived only in the West. One of her kinspeople, Running Elk, had been killed by one just a year or so ago.

He nodded. "Far from the West. From the place where there is big water. From the ocean."

"How far is that?"

"Far? I cannot tell. Many moons upon the road."

"You count by moons. Are you of my people?"

"No, I don't think so. Were it not for the sun, my skin is white. I met some of your people, hunting buffalo. They were the first people other than my own I had ever seen. I had not known there were other people. There were only robots, running wild."

She made a motion of disdain. "We have no traffic with the robots."

"So I understand."

"How much farther do you intend to go? To the east the prairie ends. It is only woods. Finally there is another ocean. I have seen the maps."

He pointed at the house that stood on top of the great headland. "Maybe only that far. The people on the plains told me of a big house of stone with people living in it. I have seen many houses of stone, but with no one living in them. There are people living in it?"

"Two people."

"That is all?"

"The others," she said, "have gone to the stars."

"They told me that, too," he said, "and I have wondered of it. I could not believe. Who would want to go to the stars?"

"They find other worlds and live on them."

"The stars are only bright lights shining in the sky."

"They are other suns," she said. "Have you read no books?"

He shook his head. "I saw one once. I was told it was a book. It was said to me that it would speak to me if one knew the way. But the person who showed it to me had lost the way."

"You cannot read?"

"This reading is the way? The way a book will talk?"

"Yes, that's it," she said. "There are little marks. You read the marks."

"Have you got a book?" he asked.

"A big box of books. I have read them all. But up there," she gestured at the house, "there are rooms filled with nothing but books. My grandfather-many-times-removed will ask today if I may read those books."

"It is strange," he said. "You read the book. I

kill the bear. I do not like the idea of a book. I was
told the book would speak, but in olden magic,
better left alone."

"That is not true," she said. "You are a funny kind
of man."

"I came from far," he said, as if that might explain it. "Across high mountains, across great rivers,
across places where there is only sand and too much
sun."

"Why did you do it? Why did you come so far?"

"Something in me said go and find. It did not say
what I should find. Only go and find. No other of
my people have ever gone to find. I feel something
driving me, as if I cannot stay. When the people on
the plains tell me of this great high house of stone,
I think perhaps this is what I go to find."

"You are going up there?"

"Yes, of course," he said.

"And if it is what you set out to find, you will
stay awhile?"

"Perhaps. I do not know. The thing inside me that
drives me on will tell me. I thought awhile ago perhaps I had found what I came to find without going
to the house. The great oak changed. You made the
oak to change."

She flared in anger. "You spied on me. You sat
there, spying."

"I did not mean to spy," he said. "I was coming
up the hill as you were coming down and I saw you
at the tree. I hid so you wouldn't see me. I thought
you would not want anyone to know. So I was quiet.
I kept out of sight. I moved away, quietly, so you
wouldn't know."

"Yet you tell me."

"Yes, I tell you. The oak was changed. It was a
wondrous thing."

"How did you know the oak had changed?"

He wrinkled his brow. "I do not know. There was
the bear as well. The bear that my arrow did not kill

and yet it dropped dead at my feet. I am puzzled by all this. I do not know these things."

"Tell me, how did the oak change?"

He shook his head. "I only sensed it change."

"You should not have spied."

"I am ashamed I did. I will not speak of it."

"Thank you," she said, turning to go down the hill.

"Can I walk a way with you?"

"I go this way," she said. "You go to the house."

"I'll see you again," he said.

She went on down the hill. When finally she looked back, he still was standing there. The bear-claw necklace glittered in the sun.

5

The alien was a can of worms. It huddled among the boulders, close up against the clump of birch that grew from one side of the gorge, the trees bent and tilted to hang above the dry stream bed. Leaf-filtered sunlight shattered itself against the twisted alien and the substance of the alien's body refracted the rays so that it seemed to sit in a pool of broken rainbows.

Jason Whitney, sitting on a mossy bank, leaned back against a small ash tree, settling himself comfortably, letting himself relax. The faint, delicate smell of dying autumn leaves filled the glen.

It was a horror, he thought, and then tried to erase the horror from his mind. Some of them weren't bad; others of them were. This was the worst he had ever seen. If it would just be still, he thought, so a man could familiarize himself with it and thus become at least partially accustomed to it. But it wouldn't be still, it kept moving that can of worms around, the movement serving to emphasize its repulsiveness.

He started to put out his mind cautiously, reaching out to touch it, then, suddenly frightened, pulled back his mind and tucked it securely inside himself.

39

He had to settle down before he tried to talk with this thing. An old alien hand like himself, he thought, should be up to almost anything, but this one had him down.

He sat quietly, smelling the dying leaves in the secluded silence, not letting himself think of much of anything at all. That was the way you did it— you sneaked up on it somehow, pretending not to notice.

But the alien didn't wait. It reached out and touched him with a mental probe that was firm and calm and warm, totally unlike the visual image of the thing.

—Welcome, it said, to this snug retreat. I trust I violate no convention in addressing myself to you and that I do not trespass. I know what you are. I have seen another of you, You are a human creature.

—Yes, said Jason, I am human. And you are most welcome here. You violate no convention, for we have few of them. And you do not trespass.

—You are one of the travelers, said the can of worms. You rest on your planet now, but at times you travel far.

—Not I, said Jason. Some of the others have, but I stay at home.

—Then truly I have arrived at my destination. This is the planet of the traveler I communicated very far ago. I could not be sure.

—This is the planet Earth, said Jason.

—That is the designation, said the creature, happily. I could not recall it. This other described it to me and I sought it far and wide, having only a general idea of the direction that it lay. But I was sure when I arrived that it was the proper planet.

—You mean you sought our Earth? You aren't simply stopping off to rest?

—I came to seek a soul.

—You came to seek a what?

—A soul, the creature said. This other one I communicated with said that humans once had souls and probably still did have them, although he could not be sure, professing much ignorance of the matter. He piqued my interest with what he told of souls, but could give me no adequate idea of what a soul might be. I say to myself, quite secretly, of course, so wonderful a thing is worth the seeking of. So I began my search.

—It might interest you to know, said Jason, that many humans have sought their souls as assiduously as do you.

And, he wondered, by what strange combination of circumstances one of the clan might have come to talk with this creature about the concept of the soul. Surely not a likely topic, he told himself, and one in which there might be certain dangers. But more than likely it had not been serious talk, or certainly had not been meant to be, although this can of worms seemed to have taken it seriously enough to send it on a search of no one could guess how many years to track it to its source.

—I sense a strangeness in your presence, the alien said. Can you tell me if you have a soul?

—No, I can't, said Jason.

—Surely if you had one, you'd be aware of it.

—Not necessarily, Jason told it.

—You sound, the creature said, very much like that one of your kind I sat with an entire afternoon on a hilltop of my own most lovely planet. We talked of many things, but the last half of our talk had much to do with souls. He didn't know if he had one, either, and was not sure that other humans had, now or in the past, and he could not tell me what a soul was or how a being, not having one, might go about the acquisition of a soul. He seemed to think he was acquainted with the advantages of possessing one, but I thought his talk on that point was somehow very hazy. It was, in many ways, a most unsatisfactory explanation that he gave me, but I thought I could detect a germ of truth in it. Surely, I thought, if I could win my way to his native planet there would be someone there who could supply the information that I seek.

—I am sorry, Jason said. Terribly sorry that you came so far and wasted so much time.

—There is nothing you can tell me? There is no one else?

—There might be, Jason told him, adding quickly, I can't be really sure.

He made a slip and knew it. He couldn't turn Hezekiah loose on a thing like this. Loopy as Hezekiah was, he would go hog wild.

—But there must be others.

—There are only two of us.

—You must be mistaken, said the alien. There were two others came. Neither one was you. They stood and looked at me and then they went away. They did not notice when I tried to communicate.

—They could not hear you, Jason said. They could not have answered. They use their minds for other things. They were the ones who told me. They knew I could talk with you.

—Then there only is one other who can communicate.

—That is all. The rest of us are gone, far among the stars. It was one of them who you talked with.

—This other one?

—I do not know, said Jason. She has never talked with people other than her own. She talks well with them, no matter how distant they may be.

—Then you are the only one. And you can tell me nothing.

—Look, said Jason, it is an old idea. There was never any proof. There was only faith. I have a soul, one would tell himself. He believed it because he had been told by others. Told authoritatively. Without any question. He was told so often and he told himself so often that there was no question in his mind that he had a soul. But there was never any evidence. There was never any proof.

—But honored sir, the alien pleaded, you will tell me, will you not, what a soul might be.

—I can tell you, Jason said, what it is supposed to be. It is a part of you. Unseen and undetectable. Not of your body. Not even of your mind. It lives on, eternally, after you are dead. Or, at least, it is supposed to live on eternally and the condition in which it finds itself once you are dead depends on what kind of creature you have been.

—Who judges what kind of creature you have been?

—A deity, said Jason.

—And this deity?

—I do not know, said Jason. I simply do not know.

—You have been honest with me, then. I must thank you most heartily for your honesty. You say much the same as the other one I talked with.

—There may be someone else, said Jason. If I can find him, I will talk with him.

—But you said . . .

—I know what I said. This is not another human. Another being that may be wiser than I am.

—I will talk with him?

—No, you cannot talk with him. There is no way you can talk with him. You'll have to leave it to me.

—I trust you, said the can of worms.

—In the meantime, said Jason, will you be my guest? I have a dwelling place. There is room for you. We would be glad to have you.

—I detect, the alien said, an uneasiness in you at the sight of me.

—I would not lie to you, said Jason. There is an uneasiness in me. But I tell myself there may be as well an uneasiness in you at the sight of me.

There was no use in lying, Jason knew. It did not take his words to tell the creature the uneasiness he felt.

—Not at all in me, the creature said. I am tolerant. But it might be best if we stay apart. I shall wait here for you.

—Is there anything you need? asked Jason. Anything you lack? Something that I could supply for nourishment or comfort?

—No, thank you. I am quite all right. I am sufficient to myself.

Jason rose and turned to leave.

—You have a lovely planet, said the alien. Such a restful place. And so filled with the strangeness of its beauty.

—Yes, said Jason, we think so, too. A very lovely planet.

He clambered up the deep-cut path he had followed down into the gorge. The sun, he saw, had passed the zenith and was slanting toward the west. Great storm clouds boiled up far off and in a little time, he knew, the sun would be hidden by them. The coming of the clouds, it seemed, had deepened the silence of the woods. He could hear the little raining sounds made by the falling leaves as they came floating down to the forest floor. Somewhere, far to the left, a squirrel was chittering, disturbed, more than likely, by some woodland fantasy that had crossed its fuzzy mind.

It had been a splendid day, he thought, a splendid day even if it rained—it still would be a splendid day in every way but one and it was a shame that it should be marred by the problem that had been thrust upon his shoulders.

To keep faith with the creature waiting in the glen, he should talk with Hezekiah, but if he talked with the self-styled robot-abbot, there was no telling what might happen. Although maybe the use of self-styled as a characterization of the robot might be a bit unfair. Who was there anymore to say that, lacking humans who were interested, robots had no grounds to assume the task of keeping alive the spark of mankind's ancient faith?

And what of that ancient faith, he wondered. Why had mankind turned away from it? It had still existed in some measure in that day when the human race had been taken elsewhere. There still were traces of it in the early writings that his grandfather had made in the first of the record books. Perhaps it existed, in a slightly different context, among the Indians, although his contact with them never had revealed it. Some, perhaps all, of the young men formed secret symbolic associations with objects in the natural world, but it was questionable that this sort of behavior could be described as any sort of faith. It was something that was never talked about and so, naturally, he had only the most meager information on it.

The wrong people had been left behind, he thought. Given another segment of the population untouched by whatever agency had carried off the human race, and the ancient human faith might still be flourishing, perhaps stronger than it had ever been. But among his people and the other people who had been in the big house above the rivers on that fateful night, the faith already had been eroded, remaining as no more than a civilized convention to which they had conformed in a lukewarm manner. There had been a time, perhaps, when it had been meaningful. In the centuries after it had been conceived in all its glory, it had been allowed to fade, to become a shadow of its former force and strength.

It had been a victim of man's mismanagement, of his overwhelming concept of property and profit. It had been manifested in lordly buildings filled with pomp and glitter rather than being nourished in the human heart and mind. And now it came to this—that it was kept alive by beings that were not even human, machines that had been accorded a measure of seeming humanness purely as a matter of man's technology and pride.

He gained the ridgetop and noticed, now that the woods fell away and his view was clear, that the storm clouds were piling ever higher in the western sky and had engulfed the sun. The house lay ahead of him and he set out toward it at a somewhat more rapid rate than he was accustomed in his walking. He had opened the record book this morning and it was still lying open on his desk, but not written in. There had been nothing to write in it this morning, but now there would be much to write—the visit of Horace Red Cloud, the alien in the glen and its strange request, the wish of Evening Star to read the books and his invitation for her to come and live with him and Martha. He would get in some writing before the hour for dinner and after the evening concert would sit down at his desk again and finish his account of the happenings of the day.

The music trees were tuning up and there was one young sapling that was doing badly. Out back a robot blacksmith was hammering noisily on metal— more than likely he was working on a plow. Thatcher, he recalled, had told him that all the plowshares had been brought in for work against the coming of the spring and another planting season.

The door off the patio opened and Martha came out and down the path toward him. She was beautiful, he thought, watching her—more beautiful, in many ways, than that long-gone day when they had been married. Their life together had been good. A man couldn't ask for better. A warm glow of thankfulness for the fullness of their life surged through him.

"Jason," she cried, hurrying to meet him. "Jason, it is John! Your brother, John, is home!"

6

(Excerpt from journal entry of September 2, 2185) . . . I often wonder how it happened we were missed. If the People were taken away, which seems far more likely than that they simply went away, by what quirk of fortune or of fate were the people in this house missed by the agency which caused the taking? The monks and brothers in the monastery a mile down the road were taken. The people in the agricultural station, a fair-sized village in itself, a half mile farther off, were taken. The great apartment complex five miles up the river, housing the workers who fished the rivers, was emptied. We alone were left.

I sometimes wonder if the social and financial privilege which had been my family's lot for the last century or more may still have been operative—that we, somehow, were above being touched even by this supernatural agency, even as we remained untouched (nay, were even benefited) by the misery and the restriction and the want which overpopulation visited upon the people of the Earth. It seems to be a social axiom that as misery and privation increase for the many, the few rise ever higher in luxury and comfort, feeding on the misery. Not aware, perhaps, that they feed upon the misery, not with any wish of feeding on it—but they do.

It is retrospective guilt, of course, which forces me to wonder this and I know it can't be true, for there were many families other than our own which fattened on the misery and they were not spared. If spared is the word. We have no idea, of course, what the taking meant. It may have meant death, or it might, as well, have spelled transference to some other place, or to many other places, and if that is true, the transference may have been a blessing. For the Earth was not, in that day, the kind of place the majority of the people would have elected to remain. The entire surface of the land, and a part of the sea as well, and the entire output of energy were utilized to maintain a bare existence for the hordes that peopled Earth. Bare existence is no idle phrase, for the people barely had enough to eat, barely room enough to live, barely fabric enough to cover their bodies for the sake of decency.

That my family, and other similar families, were allowed the privilege of retaining the relatively large amounts of living space they had fashioned for themselves well before the population pinch became as bad as it eventually became, is only one example of the inequities that existed. That the Leech Lake Indian tribe, which also was missed by the supernatural agency, had been living in a relatively large and uncrowded space can be explained in another way. The land into which they had been forced, centuries before, was largely worthless land, although throughout the years the original tract had been taken from them, bit by bit, by the relentless force of economic pressure and eventually all of it would have been taken and they would have been shoved into the anonymity of the global ghetto. Although, truth to tell, their lives had been, in some ways, a ghetto from the start.

At the time of the disappearance, the building of this house and the acquisition of the estate which surrounds it would have been impossible. For one thing, no such tract could have been found and even had it been available its price would have been such that even the most affluent of the families would not have been able to afford it. Furthermore, there would not have been the labor force or the materials available to construct the house, for the world economy was stretched to the breaking point to maintain eight billion people.

My great-grandfather built this house almost a century and a half ago. Even then the land was hard to come by and he was only able to obtain it because the monastery down the road had fallen on hard times and was forced to sell a part of its holdings to meet certain pressing obligations. In building the house, my great-grandfather ignored all modern trends and went back to the solidity and simplicity of the great country houses of some centuries before. He built it well and he often said that it would stand forever and while this, of course, was an exaggeration, there is no question that it still will stand at a time when many other buildings have crumbled into mounds.

In our present situation we are fortunate to have such a house, so solid and so large. It even now accommodates the sixty-seven persons who are resident in it without any great inconvenience, although as our population grows we may have to look for other places where some of us can live. The habitations at the agricultural station now have fallen into disrepair, but the monastery buildings, much more stoutly built, are possibilities (and the four robots who now occupy them could make do with lesser space), and the great apartment complex up the river is another lesser possibility. The apartment buildings stand in some need of repair, having stood unoccupied all these fifty years, but our corps of robots, properly supervised, should be equal to the task.

Our livelihood is well taken care of, for we have simply taken over as much as we need of the great expanse of farmland formerly worked by the agricultural station. The robots form a work force that is fully equal to the situation and as the agricultural machines broke down beyond the possibility of repair, we have gone back to farming with horses for motive power and to the simple plow, mower and reaper, which our robots have built by cannibalizing the more modern and sophisticated implements.

We are now on what I like to think of as a manorial basis—the manor providing all those things of which we have any need. We have great flocks of sheep for wool and mutton, a dairy herd for milk, beef cattle for meat, hogs for pork and ham and bacon, poultry for eggs and eating, bees and cane for honey and for sorghum, grains for flour and extensive gardens to furnish a great array of vegetables. It is a simple existence and a quiet and most satisfactory one. There were times, to start with, when we missed the old life—or at least some of the younger people missed it, but now I believe that all of us are convinced that, in its way, the life that we have fashioned is a most satisfactory one.

I have one deep regret. I have wished many times that my son, Jonathan, and his lovely wife, Marie, the parents of our three grandchildren, might have lived to be here with us. The two of them, I know, would have enjoyed the life that we live now. As a boy Jonathan never wearied of tramping over the estate. He loved the trees and flowers, the few wild creatures that managed to still exist in our little patch of woodland, the free and uncluttered feeling that a little open space could give. Now the world (or all of it I know, and I suppose the rest of it) is going back into wilderness. Trees are growing on the old farmlands. Grass has crept into places where no grass had grown before. The wild flowers are coming back and spreading from the little, forgotten nooks where they had hidden out, and the wildlife is taking over. The river valleys, now fairly heavily wooded, swarm with squirrel and coon and occasionally there are deer, probably drifting down out of the north. I know of five covey of quail that are doing well and the other day I ran into a flock of grouse. Once again the migratory wildfowl each spring and fall fly in great Vs across the sky. With man's heavy hand lifted off the Earth the little, humble creatures are coming back into an olden heritage. With certain modifications, the situation is analogous to the extinction of the dinosaurs at the close of the Cretaceous. The one important modification, of course, is that all the dinosaurs became extinct and there are a few humans still surviving. I may, however, be coming to a conclusion concerning this modification somewhat early. Triceratops, it is believed, may have been the last of the dinosaurs to disappear and it is entirely possible that small herds of Triceratops may have dragged out an existence spanning perhaps half a million years or more after the other dinosaurs had died before they, too, succumbed to the factors that had brought extinction to the others. In this light, the fact that a few hundred humans, the ragged remnants of a once mighty race, still exist may be of slight significance. We may be the Triceratops of the human species.

When the dinosaurs and many of the other reptiles died out, the mammals, which had existed in unknown numbers for millions of years, swarmed into the vacuum left by the dying reptiles and proliferated to take their place. Is this, then, another case of wiping out a certain mammalian population to give the other vertebrates a second chance, to lift from them the doom of man? Or is this facet of the situation only incidental? Has mankind, or the most of mankind, been removed to make way for a further evolutionary development? And if this should be the case, what and where is this new evolutionary creature?

What bothers one when he thinks of this is the strange process of extinction. A change in climate, a shifting of geography, disease, a scrambling of ecological parameters, factors that limit the food supply—all of these are physically, biologically and geologically understandable. The extinction, or the near extinction, of the human race is not. Slow, gradual extinction is one thing, instantaneous extinction is another. An instantaneous extinction postulates the machination of an intelligence rather than a natural process.

If the extinction were the result of the operation of another intelligence, one finds himself forced to ask not only where and what is this other intelligence, but more importantly, what could have been its purpose?

Is all life in the galaxy watched over by some great central intelligence that is alert to certain crimes that cannot be tolerated? Was the vanishing of the human race a punishment, an extermination, a death sentence passed because of what we'd done to planet Earth and to all the other creatures that had shared it with us? Or was it simply a removal, a cleansing— an action taken to ensure that a valuable planet would not be ruined utterly? Or, perhaps, in an even more far-reaching purpose, to give the planet a chance to replenish, over the next billion years or so, the natural resources of which it had been stripped—so that new coal fields might be laid down and new pools of oil created, so that ravaged soil could be rebuilt, new iron deposits come into being?

There is little purpose, I suppose, and less profit, to think of these things and to ask these questions. But man, being what he is, having obtained his short-lived dominance of the planet by virtue of his question-asking, will not be denied such speculation . . .

7

Half the afternoon the thick cloud bank had piled up in the sky and Hezekiah, watching as it climbed, had told himself that it were as if there were a ladder in the sky and the clouds had kept climbing it, growing taller and higher and more threatening and impressive as they climbed. Then, almost immediately, he had rebuked himself for thinking so—for there was no ladder, it was God's will that the clouds came climbing. He was puzzled and ashamed at these flights of fancy, at this romanticism, which he should have conquered long ago, but which, in the last few years (or so it seemed) had come welling more often to the surface. Or was it, he wondered, that only in the last few years he had directed his attention the more to these flights of fancy, aghast that there could linger in him such foolish notions, so far afield from the serious considerations to which he should be dedicated.

In the study the other brothers were bent above the books. They had sat thus for years, dedicated to the task of collating and condensing down to elemental truths all that the creature, man, had written, all that he had thought and reasoned and speculated in the spiritual sense. Of the four of them only he, Hezekiah, had not tied himself to the written or the printed word, and that had been according to the agreement they had made, in that time long centuries past when they had planned their search of truth. Three of them studying all that had been written—rewriting it, reassembling it, reassessing it, as if one man, and one man alone, had thought it all and written all of it as a single body, not many men who strove to understand, but one man who had truly understood. Three of them to do their work and the fourth who read their evaluations and assessments and, from this basis, try to puzzle out the meaning that had escaped the grasp of man. It had been a glorious idea, Hezekiah reassured himself; it had seemed so sound and it still was sound, but the way to truth was longer and more difficult than they had imagined and they still held no real inkling of the truth. Faith was something else; through the years their faith had deepened and been strengthened by their work, but the deepening of faith had not led the way to truth. Could it be possible, Hezekiah asked himself, that there was no room for both the faith and truth, that they were mutually exclusive qualities that could not coexist? He shuddered as he thought of it, for if this should be the case, they had spent their centuries of devotion to but little purpose, pursuing a will-o'-the-wisp. Must faith be exactly that, the willingness and ability to believe in the face of a lack of evidence? If one could find the evidence, would then the faith be dead? If that were the situation, then which one did they want? Had it been, he wondered, that men had tried what they even now were trying and had realized that there was no such thing as truth, but only faith, and being unable to accept the faith without its evidence, had dropped the faith as well? There was nothing in the books to make one think this might be so, but while they had thousands of books, they did not have them all. Was there somewhere in the world, moldering away, or perhaps already moldered, a book (or several books) that would make it clear what man had really done, or had tried to do and failed.

He had been pacing in the garden all the afternoon and this was not unusual, for he often walked there. Pacing helped him think and, besides, he loved the garden for the beauty that was in it—the changing of the leaves and the flowering of the blooms in season, the miracle of life and death, the singing of the birds and the pattern of their flight, the haze of the river hills, and at times, the orchestration of the music trees—although he was not sure he approved entirely of the music trees. But now he went to the door of the chapter house and as he reached it, the storm broke, great sheets of rain sweeping across the garden, pounding on the roofs, filling the gutters, the walks almost instantly transformed into brimming creeks.

He opened the door and ducked inside, but stood within the entryway a moment, holding the door partly open to gaze out across the garden, swept by the torrents of rain that came down hissing against the grass and flowers. The ancient willow tree that stood beside the bench strained in the direction of the wind, as if it were trying to tug free of the roots that anchored it.

Somewhere something was banging and as he listened, he finally made out what it was. The great metal gate that stood in the outer wall had been forced open by the wind and was banging back and forth against the field stone wall. If it were not shut and fastened, it might beat itself to pieces.

Hezekiah stepped out of the door and closed it behind him. As he went down the brimming walk, the wind and water beat at him, sluicing off his body in streaming sheets. The walk turned the corner of the building and now he walked into the wind and it was as if a great hand had been placed against his metal chest and pushed to hold him back. His brown robe trailed behind him, snapping in the wind.

The gate was straight ahead, swinging through its hinged arc and slamming against the wall, the metal shuddering at each impact with the stone. It was not only the gate that caught his attention. Lying near the gate was a sprawled and huddled shape, half on the walk, half lying on the grass. Even through the blur of rain he could make out that it was a man.

The figure lay upon its face and when he turned it over he saw the jagged cut that started at the temple and ran down across the face, not bleeding, for the rain washed the blood away, but a livid streak of torn flesh.

He got his arms around the body and stood, lifting the man from where he lay, turning and moving back along the path, driving his feet hard against the ground to brake himself against the pressure of the wind which, if he had not fought against it, would have driven him at a headlong pace.

He reached the door of the chapter house and went in. With his heel, he kicked the door shut and went across the room to a bench against the wall and laid the man upon it. He saw that the man still breathed, his chest rising and falling. He was a young man, or seemed a young man, naked except for a breech clout and a necklace of bear claws and a pair of binoculars hung around his neck.

A stranger, Hezekiah thought, a human being who had come out of nowhere and who, by the grace of God, had sought refuge in this place against the breaking storm, only to be caught and knocked unconscious by the wildly swinging gate once he had unlatched it.

This was the first time in all the years the robots had occupied the monastery that a human had ever come to this house for shelter and for aid. And that, he told himself, was mete, for historically such a place as this had stood for many centuries as a place of aid and refuge. He felt a shiver running through him, a shiver of excitement and of dedication. It was a charge they must accept, a duty and an obligation that must be fulfilled. There must be blankets to keep the young man warm, hot food, a fire, a bed—and there was in this place no such things as blankets or hot food or fires. There had not been for many years, for robots did not need them.

"Nicodemus," he shouted. "Nicodemus!"

His shouts boomed between the walls, as if olden echoes had been magically awakened, echoes that had waited for many, many years.

He heard their running feet and a door burst open and they came running through.

"We have a guest," said Hezekiah. "He is hurt and we must care for him. Run, one of you, to the House and find Thatcher. Tell him we need food and blankets and a way of making fire. Another one of you break up some of the furniture and lay it in the fireplace. All the wood we might find outdoors is wet. But try to choose the pieces that have the lesser value. Some old stools, perhaps, a broken table or a chair."

He heard them leave, heard the outer door bang as Nicodemus plunged out into the storm to go up to the House.

Hezekiah hunkered down beside the bench and kept his eyes upon the man. The breathing was regular and the face had lost some of its pallor, which had showed even through the tan. With no rain to wash it off, blood was oozing from the cut and running down the face. Hezekiah gathered up one corner of his rain-soaked robe and gently wiped it off.

Inside himself he sensed a deep, abiding peace, a sense of accomplishment, a compassion for and a dedication to this man who lay upon the bench. Was this, he wondered, the true function of the people—or the robots—who might dwell within this house? Not the vain unraveling of truth, but the succor of one's fellow men? Although that was not entirely true, he knew—not the way he said it. For this was not a fellow man lying on the bench, could not be a fellow man; a robot was not fellow to a man. But if a robot stood in place of man, if he took the place of man, if he followed in man's ways and tried to carry on the task that man had dropped, might he not, in some measure, be fellow to humanity?

And was aghast.

How could he think, even by the most clever argument, that a robot could be fellow to a man?

Vanity, he cried inside himself. An overweening vanity would be the death of him—the damnation of him, and was aghast again, for how could a robot think he was worthy even of damnation?

He was nothing and a nothing and a nothing. And yet he aped a man. He wore a robe, he sat when there was no need of either robe or sitting; he fled a storm and there was no need for such as he to flee the wet and rain. He read the books that man had written and sought an understanding that man had failed to find. He worshiped God—and that, he thought, might be the greatest blasphemy of them all.

He hunkered on the floor, close beside the bench, the sorrow and the horror welling up in him.

8

He would not have known his brother, Jason told himself, if he'd met him unaware. The stature was there and the proud, hard bearing, but the face was hidden behind a dull and grizzled beard. There was something else as well—a coldness in the eyes, a tenseness in the face. Age had not mellowed John; it had tempered and toughened him and given him a sadness that had not been there before.

"John," he said and stopped just inside the doorway. "John, we have so often wondered . . ." and then stopped talking, staring at this stranger in the room.

"It's all right, Jason," said his brother. "Martha didn't know me, either. I have changed."

"I would have," Martha said. "Given just a little time, I would have. It's the beard."

Jason went quickly across the room, grasped his brother's outstretched hand, put an arm around his shoulders and drew him close, holding him hard. "It's good to see you," he said. "So good to have you back. It has been so long."

They stepped away from one another and stood for a moment, silent, staring at one another, each trying to see in the other man the man they had seen at their last meeting. Finally, John said, "You look well, Jason. I knew I'd find you well. You always were one to look after yourself. And you have Martha, who looks after you. Some of the others that I met told me you had stayed home."

"Someone had to," Jason told him. "It was not a hardship. We have made a good life. We've been happy here."

"I asked about you often," Martha said. "I always asked about you. No one seemed to know."

"I've been far out," said John. "Out toward the center. There was something out there that I had to find. I went farther toward the center than any of the others. There were others who told me what was out there, or rather what might be out there, for they did not really know, and it seemed someone should go and see, and none of these others were about to go. Someone had to go. Someone had to go just as someone had to stay at home."

"Let's sit down," said Jason. "There's a lot you have to tell us, so let's be comfortable while you're telling it. Thatcher will bring in something and we can sit and talk. You are hungry, John?"

His brother shook his head.

"A drink, perhaps. All the old stuff's gone, but some of our robots are handy with moonshine of a sort. Properly aged and cared for, it is not too bad. We've tried to make wine, but this is not wine country. The soil's not right and the sun's not hot enough. It always turns out poor."

"Later on," said John. "After I have told you. Then we can have a drink."

"You went out to find the evil," Jason said. "That must be it. We know there's an evil out there. We got word of it quite some years ago. No one knew what it was—not even that it's really evil. All they knew was it had an evil smell."

"Not an evil," John told him. "Something worse than evil. A great uncaring. An intellectual uncaring. An intelligence that has lost what we think of as humanity. Perhaps not lost it, for it may have never had it. But that's not all of it. I found the People."

"The People!" Jason cried. "You can't mean that. No one ever knew. No one had the least idea . . ."

"Of course, no one ever knew. But I found them. They are on three planets, the planets close to one another, and they are doing very well, perhaps somewhat too well. They haven't changed. They are the same as they were five thousand years ago. They have followed to its logical conclusion the course we all were following five thousand years ago and now they are coming back to Earth. They are on their way to Earth."

A sudden wall of water slashed against the windows, driven by a wind that went howling in the eaves, far overhead.

"I do believe," said Martha, "that the storm has broken. It may be a bad one."

9

She sat and listened to the voices of the books—
or, rather, perhaps, to the voices of the men who had
written all the books, strange, grave voices far off
in time, speaking from the depths of time, the distant mumble of many cultivated voices, without
words, but with meaning and with thought instead of
words, and she had never thought, she told herself,
it could be anything like this. The trees had words
to speak and the flowers a meaning and the little
people of the woods often talked to her and the
river and the running streams had music and a magic
that surpassed understanding. But this was because
they were living things—yes, even the river and the
brook could be thought of as living things. Could it
be that books were living, too?

She had never known there could be so many
books, a large room, floor to ceiling, lined with rows
of books, and many times that number, she had been
told by the funny little robot, Thatcher, stored away
in basement rooms. But the strangest thing of all was
that she could think of a robot as being a funny sort
of creature—almost as if he were a man. No great
black horror that stalked the evening skyline, no
midnight wraith out of the place of dreams; if not
a man at least a manlike being with a gentle voice.

Perhaps it had been something he had said: "Here you can trace and chart the path of man up from darkest night." Saying it proudly, as if he were a man himself and alone, in terror and in hope, had trod that very path.

The voices of the books kept mumbling in the dimness of the room while rain ran down the windows—a companionable muttering that must keep on forever, the ghostly conversations of long-dead writers whose works lined the study walls. Was it all imagination, she asked herself, or did others hear them, too—did Uncle Jason sometimes hear them as he sat here by himself? Although she knew, even as she wondered it, that this was something she could never ask. Or could it be heard by no one but herself, hearing it as she had heard the voice of Old Grandfather Oak on that long-gone summer day before the tribe had gone into the wild rice country, as she this very day had sensed the lifting of the arms and the benediction?

As she sat there, at a small desk in one corner of the room, with the book opened on the desk (not the big desk where Uncle Jason sat to write the chronicles), listening to the wind running in the eaves, watching the rain sluice down the windows from which Thatcher had drawn the drapes with the passing of the morning sun, she moved into another place, or seemed to move into another place, although the room remained. In this place were many people, or at least the shadows of many people, and many other desks and far distant times and places, although the distance of the times and places seemed less than they should have been, as if the veils of time and space had grown very thin and were ready to dissolve, so that she sat, an observer to a great event—the running together of all time and space so that the both of them became almost nonexistent, no longer caging men and events into separate cells, but running them all together, as if everything had happened all at once and in the self-same area, with the past crowding close upon the future within the confines of a tiny point of existence that, for convenience, might be called the present. Frightened at what was happening, she nevertheless glimpsed for a terrible, sublime moment all the causes and effects, all the direction and the purpose, all the agony and glory that had driven men to write all the billions of words that stood stacked within the room. Glimpsed it all without understanding, with no time or capacity for an understanding, understanding only that what had happened in the minds of men to drive them to create all the mumbled, scribbled, burning words had not been so much the work of many individual minds as the impact of a pattern of existence upon the minds of all mankind.

The spell. (if it were no more than a spell) was broken almost immediately, with Thatcher coming through the door and padding across the room toward her, carrying a tray which he put down upon the desk.

"This is slightly delayed, miss," he apologized. "Just as I was about to bring it Nicodemus from the monastery came rushing in to say that hot soup and blankets and many other things were needed for the comfort of an injured pilgrim."

A glass of milk, a jar of wild gooseberry jam, slices of buttered bread and a slab of honey cake rested on the tray. "It is not elaborate," said Thatcher. "It is not as splendid as a guest of this house has reason to expect, but taking care of the monastery's needs, I did not have the time to do full justice to it."

"It is more than adequate," said Evening Star. "I had not expected such a kindness. Busy as you were, you should not have bothered."

"Miss," said Thatcher, "through the centuries it has been my pleasure and responsibility to operate this household according to certain standards that have not varied through all the days of my stewardship. I am only sorry that the procedure should, for the first time, have been upset on your first day here."

"Never mind," she told him. "You said a pilgrim. Do pilgrims often come to the monastery? I have never heard of them."

"This one," Thatcher said, "is the first there ever was. And I am not sure that he is a pilgrim, although that is what Nicodemus called him. A mere wanderer, no doubt, although that is memorable in itself, for never before has there been a human wanderer. A young man, almost naked, as Nicodemus tells it, with a bear-claw necklace encircling his throat."

She sat stiff and straight, remembering the man who had stood that morning on the bluff top with her.

"Is he badly hurt?" she asked.

"I do not think so," Thatcher told her. "He sought refuge in the monastery from the storm. When he opened the gate, the wind caught it and it struck him. He is very much alive."

"He is a good man," said Evening Star, "and a very simple man. He cannot even read. He thinks the stars are no more than points of light shining in the sky. But he can sense a tree . . ."

And stopped, confused, for she must not talk about the tree. She must learn to guard her tongue.

"Miss, you know this human?"

"No. I mean I do not know him. I saw him for a moment and talked with him this morning. He said he was coming here. He was seeking something and thought he might find it here."

"All humans seek for something," Thatcher said. "We robots are quite different. We are content to serve."

10

"To begin with," said John Whitney, "I simply wandered. It was wonderful to all of us, of course, but I think, somehow, most wonderful of all to me. The idea that man could be a free agent in the universe, that he could go wherever he might wish, was a bit of magic that was utterly beyond all comprehension, and that he could do this by himself, with no machinery, with no instruments, with nothing but his body and his mind, through a power that he held within himself and which no human had ever known before, was simply unbelievable, and I found myself exercising the power to prove to myself again and yet again that it could be really done, that it was a solid and ever-present ability that could be called upon at will and that it was never lost, and that it belonged to one by right of his humanity and not by some special dispensation that could be withdrawn at a moment's notice. You never tried it, Jason, neither you nor Martha?"

Jason shook his head. "We found something else. Not as exhilarating, perhaps, but with a deep satisfaction of its own. A love of land and a feeling of continuity, a sense of heritage, even of being a substantial part of that heritage, an earthbound certainty."

"I think I can understand that," said John. "It's something that I never had and I suspect it was the lack of it that drove me on and on once the sheer exuberance of traveling from one star to another had worn somewhat thin. Although I still can become excited over a new place that I find—for there are never any of them that are exactly like another. The one amazing thing to me, the thing that continues to amaze me, is the great range of dissimilarities that can exist, even on those planets where the basic characteristics of their geology and history are very much the same."

"But why did you wait so long, John? All these years without coming home. Without letting us know. You said you had met others and that they told you we were still on Earth, that we had never left."

"I had thought of it," said John. "Many times I thought of it, of coming back to see you. But I'd have come back empty-handed, with not a thing to show for all the years of wanderlust. Not possessions, of course, for we know now they don't count. But nothing really learned, no great new understanding. A fistful of stories of where I'd been and what I'd seen, but that would have been the size of it. The prodigal coming home and I . . ."

"But it wouldn't have been that way. Your welcome always waited you. We've waited for years and asked of you."

"What I don't understand," said Martha, "is why there was no word of you. You said you had met others and I talk all the time with our people out there and there never was a word about you, never any news. You just dropped out of sight."

"I was far out, Martha. Much farther than most of the others ever got. I ran hard and fast. Don't ask me why. I sometimes asked myself and there was never any answer. Never any real answer. The others that I met, only two or three of them quite by accident, had run as hard as I. Like a bunch of kids,

I suppose, who come to a new and wondrous place, and there is so much to see they're afraid they'll not get to see it all, so they run hard to see it all, telling themselves that once they've seen it all, they'll go back to the one place that is best, probably knowing that they never will, for that one best place is always, in their minds, just a little way ahead and they become obsessed with the idea that if they don't keep going they will never find it. I knew what I was doing and I knew it made no sense and it was some comfort to me when I met those other few who were the same as I."

"But there was purpose in your running," Jason said. "Even if you didn't know it at the time, the purpose still was there. For you found the People. If you hadn't gone so far, I don't suppose you'd ever have found them."

"That is true," said John, "but I had no sense of purpose. I simply stumbled on them. I had no word of them, no inkling they were there. I wasn't hunting them. I had sensed the Principle and I was hunting it."

"The Principle?"

"I don't know how I can tell you, Jason. There aren't words to tell you. There is no way I can express exactly what it is, although I am certain I have a fairly good idea. Perhaps no man can ever know exactly what it is. You remember that you said there was an evil toward the center. That evil is the Principle. The people I met far out had sensed it, too, and somehow must have sent back word. But evil is not right; it is not really evil. Sensed, scented, become aware of from far off, it has the smell of evil because it is so different, so unhuman, so uncaring. By human standards blind and reasonless, and seeming blind and reasonless because there is about it not one single emotion, one single motive or purpose, one single thought process that can be equated with the human mind. A spider is blood brother and intellectual equal to us as compared to it. It sits there and it knows. It knows all there is to know. And its knowing is translated in such nonhuman terms that we could never even scratch the surface of the simplest of those terms. It sits there and knows and translates what it knows and that translation of its knowledge is so coldly correct that one shrinks away from it, for there is nothing that can be so right, without the slightest possibility of error. I've said it is unhuman and perhaps it is this ability to be so utterly right, so absolutely correct, that makes it so unhuman. For proud as we may be of our intellect and understanding, there is no one of us who can say with any honesty or any certainty that he is correct on any point of information or interpretation."

"But you said that you found the People and they're coming back to Earth," said Martha. "Can't you tell us more about them and when they're coming back . . ."

"My dear," said Jason, softly, "I think there's more that John wants to tell us, that he has to tell us before he talks about the People."

John rose from the chair in which he had been sitting, walked to the rain-smeared window and looked out, then came back to face the two sitting on the davenport. "Jason is right," he said. "There is more I have to tell. I've wanted for so long to tell it to someone, to share it all with someone. I may be wrong. I've thought about it for so long that I may have become confused. I'd like to have you two hear me out and tell me what you think."

He sat down on the chair again. "I'll try to present it as objectively as I can," he said. "You realize that I never saw this thing, this Principle. I may not have even gotten close to it. But close enough to know that it is there and to sense a little, perhaps as much as any man may sense, the sort of thing it is. Not understanding it, of course, not even trying to understand it, for you know you are too small and weak for understanding. That was the thing that hurt the most, perhaps—realizing how small and weak you were, and not only you yourself, but all humanity. Something that reduced the human race to microbe status, perhaps to less than microbe status. You know instinctively that you, as one human being, are beneath its notice, although there is evidence, or I think there may be evidence, that it could and did take notice of humanity.

"I got as close to it as my mind could bear. I cowered before it. I don't know what else I did. There is a part of all of this that tends to go foggy in the mind. Perhaps I got too close. But I had to know, you see. I had to be sure and I am sure. It is out there and it watches and it knows and if need be it can act, although I am inclined to think it would not be quick to act . . ."

"Act—how?" asked Jason.

"I don't know," John told him. "You have to understand this is all impression. Intellectual impression. Nothing visual. Nothing that I saw or heard. It's the fact that it's all intellectual impression that makes it so hard to describe. How do you describe the reactions of the human mind? How do you blueprint the emotional impact of those reactions?"

"We had the report," Jason said to Martha. "You picked it up from someone. Do you remember who it was, who it might have been who was out as far as John, or almost as far as John . . ."

"They wouldn't have had to be out as far as I was," said John. "They could have picked up the sense of it a good deal farther off. I deliberately tried to get in close to it."

"I don't remember who it was," said Martha. "Two or three people told me of it. It was, I'm sure, all very second-hand. Maybe tenth- or twelfth-hand. Word that had been passed on from one person to another, from many persons to many other persons. Simply that there was something evil out near the center of the galaxy. That someone had been out there and had run into it. But no hint that anyone had investigated. Afraid to investigate, perhaps."

"That would be right," said John. "I was very much afraid."

"You call it a Principle," said Jason. "That is a funny thing to call it. Why the Principle?"

"It was what I thought when I was close to it," said John. "It didn't tell me. It didn't communicate at all. It probably was not even aware of me, didn't know that I existed. One tiny little microbe creeping up on it . . ."

"But Principle? It was a thing, a creature, an entity. That is a strange designation to hang on a creature or an entity. There must have been a reason."

"I'm not sure, Jason, that it is a creature or an entity. It is simply something. A mass of intelligence, perhaps. And what form would a mass of intelligence take? What would it look like? Could you even see it? Would it be a cloud, a wisp of gas, trillions of tiny motes dancing in the light of the center's suns. And the reason for calling it the Principle? I can't really tell you. There is no logic to it, no single reason I can put a finger on. Simply that I felt it was the basic principle of the universe, the director of the universe, the brain center of the universe, the thing that holds the universe together and makes it operate—the force that makes the electrons spin about the nucleus, that makes the galaxies rotate about their centers, that holds everything in place."

"Could you pinpoint its location?" Jason asked.

John shook his head. "No way that I could. No such thing as triangulation. The feel of the Principle was everywhere, it seemed; it came from everywhere. It closed in around you. It muffled and engulfed you; there was no sense of direction. And in any case, it would be difficult, for there are so many suns and so many planets. Jammed close together. Suns fractions of light-years apart. Old, the most of them. Most of the planets dead. Some of them with the wreckage and ruin of what at one time must have been great civilizations, but now all of them are gone . . ."

"Perhaps it was one of these civilizations . . ."

"Perhaps," said John. "I thought so at first. That one of the ancient civilizations had managed to survive and that its intelligence evolved into the Principle. But since then I've come to doubt it. For more time would have been needed, I'm convinced, than the lifetime of a galaxy could afford. I can't begin to tell you, I don't know how to tell you, the sheer force of this intelligence, or the alienness of it. Not just the difference of it. Throughout all space you find scattered intelligences that are different and these differences make them alien. But not alien in the way the Principle is alien. And this terrible alienness hints at an origin not of the galaxy, of a time before the galaxy, of a place and time so different from the galaxy that it would be inconceivable. You are acquainted, I suppose, with the theory of the steady-state?"

"Yes, of course," said Jason. "The universe had no beginning and will never have an end, that it is in a state of continual creation, new matter being formed, new galaxies coming into being even as the old ones die. But the cosmologists, before the disappearance of the People, had fairly well established that the theory was untenable."

"I know they did," said John. "But there was still one hope—you could call it hope, for there were certain people who, for philosophical reasons, clung stubbornly to the steady-state concept. It was so beautiful, so superb and awe-inspiring, that they would not let it go. And they said, suppose that the universe is far bigger than it seems to be, that what we see is only a local segment, one tiny local bubble on the skin of this greater universe and this local bubble is going through a phase that makes it appear not to be steady-state, but an evolving universe."

"And you think that they were right?"

"I think they could be right. Steady-state would give the Principle the time that it needed to come into being. Before it came into being the universe may have been chaotic. The Principle may be the engineering force that put it all to right."

"You believe all this?"

"Yes, I do believe it. I've had time to think of it and I put it all together and I did the job so well that I'm convinced of it. Not a shred of proof. Not a point of information. But it's fastened in my mind and I can't shake it free. I try to tell myself that the Principle, or certain features of the Principle, may have put it in my mind, might have planted it. I try to tell this to myself because it's the only way that I can explain it. And yet I know I must be wrong, for I am sure the Principle was entirely unaware of me. There was never any sign it was aware of me."

"You got close to it, you say."

"As close as I dared to get. I was frightened all the way. I went to a point where I had to break and run."

"Somewhere along the way you found the People. So there was purpose after all. You never would have found them if you'd not gone chasing after this thing you call the Principle."

"Jason," Martha said, "you don't sound too impressed. What's the matter with you? Here your brother has come back and . . ."

"I am sorry," Jason said. "I would suppose I do not grasp it yet. It is too big to grasp. Maybe I'm deeply horrified and calling it 'this thing' is simply a defense mechanism to hold it away from me."

"I found the same reaction in myself," John told Martha. "That is, to begin with. I soon got over it. And, yes, I'd have never found the People if I'd not tracked down the Principle. It was blind luck I found them. I had started back, you see, and was planet hopping, but going on a different tack than the one I'd followed going in. You have to be extremely careful, as I suppose you know, in choosing the planets that you use. You can sense them and pick out the ones that seem the best and there are a lot of guidelines that serve you fairly well, but there always is a chance that a planet might have some characteristics that you have not detected or lack something that you took for granted and that simply isn't there, so you have to have an alternative or two, so that if anything goes sour with the planet you have chosen you can shift most hurriedly to another one. I had alternatives and I hit a planet that, if not deadly, was uncomfortable, so I switched quickly to another one and that's where I found the People. It was still fairly close to the Principle and I wondered how they stood it, how they could live so close to it and entirely disregard it, or pretend to disregard it. I thought perhaps they had become accustomed to it, although it did not seem the sort of thing one could very readily become accustomed to. It was only after a time that I realized they were unaware of it. They had not developed parapsychic abilities, as we have, and they were entirely deaf to it. They had no idea such a thing was there.

"I was fortunate. I materialized in an open field— materialized is not the word, of course; there is no word for it. It's insane that a man can do a thing and still have no word for what he does. Do you happen to know, Jason, if anyone has actually figured out what actually happens when we go star-traveling?"

"No, I don't," said Jason. "I would think not. Martha might know better than I do. She keeps up a running conversation with the stars. She hears all the news."

"There have been those who've tried," said Martha. "They have gotten nowhere. That was earlier. I don't think anyone has bothered for a long, long time. They just accept it now. No one wonders anymore about how or why it works."

"Perhaps it's just as well," said John. "But, the situation being as it is, I could have muffed it. I could have arrived at a place that teemed with people and someone might have seen me appearing out of nothing or I, seeing humans in numbers for the first time in centuries, or somehow recognizing them as the people who had been taken, might have rushed into their arms, elated at having finally found them, although I was not looking for them. It was the last thing in my mind.

"But I arrived in an open field and at some distance I saw other humans, or what I thought were humans—farmers working with big powered agricultural implements. And when I saw the implements, I knew that if they should be humans, they'd not be humans of our kind, for we've had nothing to do with powered machines of any sort for millennia. The thought crossed my mind that if the creatures undeniably were humans, they might be the ones who were taken from the Earth and my knees went wobbly at the thought of it and I was filled with a great elation. Although I told myself that would be most unlikely and the only other alternative was that I'd found another race of humanoid creatures and that was unlikely, too, for in all the galaxy no one has ever found another human race. Or have they? I've been gone so long my information is much out of date."

"No one has," said Martha. "Many other creatures, but no humanoids."

"There was, too, the fact that they had machines. And I told myself that made the possibility even of less likelihood. For we've found new technological races and of those the technology so weird that in many cases it was impossible for us to grasp the principle or the purpose of it. To find another humanoid race with machine technology seemed to me absurd. The only answer could be that here were the People. Realizing this, I became somewhat cautious. We might be of the same blood, but there was five thousand years between us and I reminded myself that five thousand years might have made them as alien as anything we've found in space. And we've learned, if nothing else, that first contact with aliens must be managed adroitly.

"I will not try to tell you now all the things that happened. Later on, perhaps. But I rather think I managed very well. Although I guess, it was mostly luck. When I went up to the farmers I was mistaken for a wandering scholar from another of the three planets the human race inhabits—not quite right in the head and concerned with things no normal man would think worth consideration. Once I caught the drift of it, I went along with them. It covered up a lot of slips I made. My slips seemed no more than eccentricities to them. I think it may have been my clothing and my language that made them think I was a wanderer. Luckily, they spoke a sort of English, but changed considerably from the language that we speak. I would imagine that back on the old Earth of five thousand years ago our language, as we speak it now, would not be readily understood. Time and changing circumstance and sloppiness in speech brings about many changes in the spoken word. Under the guise of their mistake, I was able to get around enough to find out what was going on, to learn what sort of society had developed and some of their long-range planning."

"And," said Jason, "it turned out not so pretty."

John gave him a startled glance. "How would you know that?"

"You said they still had a machine technology. I think that might be the key. I would guess they continued, once they got themselves sorted out, in about the same way they were going before they were snatched off Earth. And if that is the case, the picture would not be a pretty one."

"You are right," said John. "It took them, apparently, not too long to get themselves, as you say, sorted out. Within a few years after finding themselves, in a twinkling, on another planet, or on other planets, rather, in an unguessed part of space, they got their bearings and became organized and went on pretty much the way they had left off. They had to start from scratch, of course, but they had the technological knowledge and they had brand-new planets with untouched raw materials and they were very quickly on their way. And what was more, they have the same life expectancy, the same long life that we have. A lot of them died in those first few years while they struggled to get themselves adjusted, but there still were a lot of them left, and among those were people with all the skills that were needed to develop a new technology. Can you imagine what might happen if a skilled, trained engineer or a well-grounded, imaginative scientist lived for many centuries? The society did not lose needed skills by death, as had been the case before. Geniuses did not die, but continued being geniuses. Engineers did not build and plan for a few years only and then die or retire, but kept on building and planning. A man with a theory was given as many centuries as he needed to develop it to its full potentiality and retained the youth that was needed to continue with it. There is a great drawback to this, of course. The presence of men of great age and vast experience and in positions of importance would tend to have an inhibiting influence upon younger men and would make for a conservatism that would be blind to new ideas and in the end would stall all progress if it had not been recognized and compensated for. The People had the sense to recognize it and to build some compensatory features into the social structure."

"Were you able to arrive at any idea of their time

table? How swiftly did they get started again and how they may have progressed?"

"Roughly. Nothing definite, of course. But say a hundred years to get themselves established as a viable society, perhaps three hundred to rebuild an approximation of the kind of technological setup they had here on Earth. And from there they built on the basis of what they had, with the advantage of being able to drop a lot of ancient millstones they carried around their necks. They build from scratch and to start with there was no need to struggle with the obsolescence they were burdened with on Earth. Well before a thousand years had passed the groups living on the three different planets—all within less than a light-year of one another—knew about the others and in a very little time spaceships had been developed and built and the human race was together once again. The physical contact and the commerce this made possible gave the technology a new shot in the arm, for during those thousand years or so they had been apart each had developed their technology a little differently, had gone probing in different directions. And also they had the resources of three planets rather than of one and that must have been a distinct advantage. What happened was the melding of three separate cultures into a sort of superculture that still had the advantage of having common roots."

"They never developed parapsychic powers? No sign of them at all?"

John shook his head. "They are as blind to them as they had been before. It's not only time that's needed to develop them, for now each of them, all of them, have as much time as we have. It must be that what is needed is a different outlook, a lifting of the pressures that a particular brand of technology imposes not only on a race, but on each human being."

"And this brand of technology?"

"To you and me," said John, "it would be brutal.

Knowing nothing else, seeing in it the goals they have striven for, it must seem wonderful to them. Satisfactory, if not wonderful. For them it represents freedom, the freedom of being lifted above and beyond the environment they have struggled to subdue and bend to their purposes; to us it would be stifling."

"But they must think back," said Martha. "Their transfer from Earth must be recent enough that it is remembered. There must be records. They must have wondered all these years what happened to them and where the Earth may be."

"Records, yes," said John. "Myth-haunted, for it was some time, many years, before anyone got around to putting anything on paper and by that time the incident had grown misty and no two men, most likely, could ever quite agree on what exactly happened. But they did think about it. It was forever in their minds. They tried to explain it and there are some marvelous theories and once again there is no agreement on one particular theory. The fuzziness of it all may seem difficult for us to understand, for you have your records, Jason, the ones Grandfather started. I suppose you keep them up."

"Sporadically," said Jason. "Often there is not much to write about."

"Our records," said John, "were written with clear deliberation, with a sense of calmness. We had no upheaval; we were simply left behind. But with the others there was upheaval. It is hard to imagine how it might have been. To be one second on familiar Earth, the next dumped on a planet that was, of course, much the same as Earth, but in many ways entirely different. To be dumped there without food, with no possessions, without shelter. To become pioneers at a moment's notice, under the most adverse circumstances. They were frightened and confused and, worst of all, entirely mystified. There is a great need for man to explain what happens to him or how a thing has happened and they had no way to arrive at any explanation. It was as if magic had been performed—a very vicious and unfeeling magic. The wonder is that any of them survived at all. Many of them didn't. And to this day they don't know why or how it happened. But I think I know the why of it, the reason. Maybe not the method, but the reason."

"You mean the Principle?"

"The idea may be no more than fantasy," said John. "I may have arrived at it because there seemed no other explanation. If the People had parapsychic abilities and knew what I know, that the Principle exists, I have no doubt they would arrive at the same idea as I have. Which wouldn't mean that we were correct. I have said that I don't think the Principle was aware of me. I'm not sure it could become aware of any single human being—it would be akin to a human being becoming aware of a single microbe. Although it may have the power to focus down to very fine perception; it may have no limitations whatever. But in any case it would be more likely to pay attention to humans in a mass, to any sort of creature in a mass, being attracted, perhaps, to the social structure and the intellectual trend brought about by such a mass of beings rather than by the mere massiveness itself. To attract its attention, I would presume that any situation would have to be unique and from what we ourselves have found so far in the galaxy, I would assume that the humanity of five millennia ago, in the full flower of its technological development and its materialistic point of view, must have seemed unique. The Principle may have studied us for a time and puzzled over us, maybe a bit apprehensive over the possibility that, given time, we could upset the orderliness and precision of the universe—which would have been something it would not have been willing to tolerate. So I think it did with us exactly what men of that day would have done if they'd found a new strain of virus that might just possibly be dangerous. Such a virus would have been placed in culture tubes and run through many tests, trying to determine what it might do under varying conditions. The Principle reached out and grabbed humanity and dumped it on three planets and then settled back to watch, wondering, perhaps, if there'd be divergence or if the strain ran true. By this time it must know that the strain runs true. The cultures on the three planets varied, certainly, but even in their variance all three were technological and materialistic, and once they became aware of one another they had no trouble pooling their characteristics to become a superculture, still materialistic, still technological."

"I don't know why," said Jason, "but when you talk about the People I have the feeling that you are describing a monstrous alien race rather than humanity. Without knowing any of the details, they sound frightening."

"They are to me," said John. "Not perhaps because of any single facet of their culture, for some of these facets can be very pleasant, but because of a sense of the irresistible arrogance implicit in it. Not the power so much, although the power is there, but the naked arrogance of a species that sees everything as property to be manipulated and used."

"And yet," said Martha, "they are our people. The rest of us have wondered about them for so long, have worried over them, wondering what could have happened to them, fearful of what had happened to them. We should be happy that we found them, happy that they have done so well."

"I suppose we should," said Jason, "but somehow I can't. If they'd stay where they are, I'd feel differently about it, I imagine. But John said they're coming back to Earth. We can't let them come. Can you imagine what it might be like? What they'd do to Earth and us?"

"We might have to leave," said Martha.

"We can't do that," said Jason. "Earth is part of us. And not only you and I, but the others, too. Earth is the tie, the anchor. It holds us together—all of us, even those who have never been on Earth."

"Why did they have to locate Earth?" asked Martha. "How could they, lost among the stars, have located Earth?"

"I don't know," said John. "But they are clever. Far too clever, more than likely. Their astronomy, all their sciences, exceed anything that man of Earth had even dared to dream. Somehow they managed to sift among the stars until they found, and identified, the old ancestral sun. And they have the ships to get here. They've gone to many other, nearby suns, exploring and exploiting."

"It may take them awhile to get here," Jason said. "We'll have some time to figure out what should be done."

John shook his head. "Not with the kind of ships they have, traveling many times the speed of light. The survey ship had been a year on its way when I found out about it. It could be here almost any time."

11

(Excerpt from journal entry of April 19, 6135) . . . Today we planted the trees that Robert brought back from one of the stars far out toward the Rim. We planted them most carefully on the little knoll halfway between the House and the monastery. The robots planted them, of course, but we were there to provide unneeded supervision, making, in effect, a quiet ceremony of it. There was Martha and myself and Robert and while we were about it, Andrew and Margaret and their children happened to drop in and Thatcher sent them out to us and we made quite a party of it.

I wonder, sitting here tonight, how the trees will thrive. It is not the first time we have tried to introduce an alien plant to the soil of Earth. There were, for example, the pocketful of cereal grains that Justin carried with him from out Polaris way and the tubers that Celia gathered in another of the Rim systems. Either one of them would have provided another welcome food plant to add to those we have, but in each case we lost them, although the grain dragged out through several seasons, producing less and less, until in the final year we planted the little that we had and it failed to germinate. There is, I suspect, lacking in our soil some vital factor, perhaps the

absence of certain minerals, or perhaps the absence
of an alien bacteria or little microscopic animal life
forms that may be necessary to the growth of alien
plants.

We shall lavish great care on the trees, of course,
and shall watch them closely, for if we can keep them
alive and thriving it will be a wondrous thing. Robert
calls them music trees and says that on their native
planet there are great groves of them and that in
the evening hours they play their concerts, although
why they should play a concert is very hard to tell,
for there lives upon this planet no other form of
life with an intellectual capacity to appreciate good
music. Perhaps they play it for themselves, or perhaps for one another, with one grove listening in
deep appreciation while its neighbor grove takes over
for the evening.

I would suspect that there might be other reasons
for the playing that Robert has not caught, being
content to sit and listen and not disposed to inquire
too deeply into the reason for the music. But when
I try to think of those other possible reasons, there
is not a single one that occurs to me. We are too
limited, of course, in our experience and history,
to attempt to understand the purposes of the other
life forms that live within the galaxy.

Robert was able to bring to Earth only a half
dozen of the trees, little saplings three feet high or
so, which he had dug most carefully, using his clothing to ball the roots, so that he arrived on Earth
quite naked. My clothes are somewhat large for him,
but being the kind of man he is, always ready to
laugh, even at himself, he does not seem to mind.
The robots are now engaged in making him a ward-
robe and he'll leave Earth much better equipped,
garmentwise, than he had been when he stripped
himself to ball the trees.

We have no reasonable expectations, of course,
that the trees will survive, but the hope they will is

good to think upon. Thinking back, it is so long since I have heard music, of any sort, that it is difficult to remember what it might be like. Neither Martha nor myself has any musical ability. Only a couple of the others of the original group had a musical sense and they are long gone from Earth. Years ago, seized with a great idea, I read enough about music to understand some of the basics of its playing and made an attempt to have the robots construct instruments, which did not turn out too well, and then to play them, which turned out even worse. Apparently the robots, or at least the ones on this farm, have no more musical ability than I. In the days of our youth most of the music was electronically recorded and since the Disappearance there has been no way in which it can be reproduced. As a matter of fact, my grandfather, realizing this, when he collected books and art, made no effort to collect any tapes, although I believe that in one of the basement vaults there is a respectable collection of musical scores, the old gentleman hoping, perhaps, that in the years to come there might be those with some musical aptitude who would find use for them . . .

12

He knew of music and was entranced by it, sometimes imagining that he heard it in the wind blowing through the trees, or in the silvery tinkling of swift water running over stones, but never in his life had he heard music such as this.

There had been Old Jose, he remembered, hunkered of an evening at the doorway of his hut, tucking the fiddle underneath his chin and drawing the bow across the strings to make happiness or sadness or sometimes neither, but just a flow of sweetness. "Although I can no longer do it well," he'd say. "My fingers no longer dance upon the strings with the nimbleness they should and my arm has grown too heavy to draw the bow with the lightness it should have. Like the wings of a butterfly across the strings —that's the way of it." But to the boy, crouching in the sand, still warm from the sun, it had been wonderful. On the high hill behind the hut a coyote would point its nose into the sky and howl accompaniment, voicing the loneliness of hill and sea and beach, as if he and the old man with the fiddle and the crouching lad were all the life still left in this lonesome land, with the stubs and mounds of ancient shapes showing in the dust of twilight.

There had been, much later, the buffalo hunters

on the plains with their drums and rattles and the
deer bone whistles, thumping out the beat to which
he and the others danced in the flickering campfire
light, dancing with a high exhilaration that he sensed
had its roots far back in time.

But this was neither fiddle nor deer bone whistle,
nor the thump of drum; this was music that filled
the world and thundered at the sky, that caught one
up and carried him, that drowned him, that made one
forgetful of his body, welding his very being into the
pattern that the music wrought.

One part of his brain was not caught, was not
drowned, but held out against the magic of the
sound in puzzled wonderment, saying over and over
to itself: It is the trees that make the music. The
little clump of trees standing on the knoll, ghostly
in the evening, so clean and fresh after the sweep
of rain, white like birch, but larger than most birch.
Trees with drum and fiddle and deer bone whistle
and much more than that, putting it all together until
the very heavens talked.

He became aware that someone had moved up the
garden and now stood beside him, but he did not turn
to see who it might be, for there was something
wrong out on the knoll. Despite all the beauty and
power there was something there that was not exactly
right, something that, if it could be fixed, would
make the music perfect.

Hezekiah reached out and gently adjusted the
bandage on the young man's cheek.

"Are you feeling all right now?" he asked. "Are
you feeling better?"

"It is beautiful," said the young man, "but there
is something wrong."

"There is nothing wrong," said Hezekiah. "We
bandaged you and kept you warm and fed you and
now you are all right."

"Not me. The trees."

"They are playing well," said Hezekiah. "They

seldom have played better. And it is one of their old pieces, not one of their experimental . . ."

"There is a sickness in them."

"Some of the trees are old and dying," Hezekiah said. "They do not perform perfectly, perhaps, not as they did in their younger days, but they still do well. And there are some young saplings that have not caught the knack."

"Why does no one help them?"

"There is no way to help them. Or if there is, no one knows of it. All things grow old and die, you from oldness, I from rust. They are not trees of Earth. They were brought here many centuries ago by one of those who travel to the stars."

And there, the young man thought, was the talk again of traveling to the stars. The buffalo hunters had told him there were men and women who traveled to the stars and again this morning the girl he had talked with had mentioned it again. Of them all, the girl might know; for she could talk with trees. Had she, he wondered, ever talked with the ghostly trees standing on the knoll?

She could talk with trees and he could kill the bears and suddenly the moment was with him once again when that last bear had reared up from the gully and had been far too close. But now, for some strange reason, it was not the bear at all, but the trees upon the knoll and in that instant the same thing happened as had happened with the bear, that same sense of going out and meeting. And the meeting of what? The bear? The trees?

Then it was all gone and he was back inside himself again and the wrongness of the trees was gone and everything was right. The music filled the world and thundered at the sky.

Hezekiah said, "You must be wrong about the trees. There can be no sickness in them. It seems to me, right now, they do as well as I ever can remember."

13

Jason woke in the night and could not go to sleep again. It was not his body that defied sleep, he knew; it was his mind, so filled with speculation, half numbed with apprehension, that it refused to rest.

Finally he got up and began to dress.

From her bed, Martha asked, "What is the matter, Jason?"

"Can't sleep," he told her. "I am going for a walk."

"Take your cape," she said. "The night wind might be chill. And try not to worry. It will work out all right."

Going down the stairs, he knew that she was wrong and knew she must be wrong; she spoke the way she did in an attempt to cheer him. It would not work out all right. When the People returned to Earth, life would be changed, it would never be the same again.

As he came out on the patio, old Bowser came wobbling around the corner of the kitchen. There was no sign of the younger dog that usually accompanied him on his walks, or of any of the others. They were either asleep somewhere or out exploring for a coon or maybe nosing out the mice from among the corn shocks. The night was quiet and slightly chilly and had at once a frosty and a melancholy feel

91

about it. A thin moon hung in the west, above the darkness of the wooded bluff across the Mississippi. The faint, sharp tang of dying leaves hung in the air.

Jason went down the path that led to the point of rocks above the meeting of the rivers. The old dog fell in behind him. The crescent moon shed but little light, although, Jason told himself, he scarcely needed light. He had walked this path so many times he could find it in the dark.

The earth was quiet, he thought, not only here, but everywhere. Quiet and resting after the turbulent centuries when man cut down its trees, ripped out its minerals, plowed its prairies, built upon broad expanses of it and fished its waters. After this short rest, would it all begin again? The ship heading for the Earth from the human planets was only an exploratory probe, to find old Earth again, to make sure the astronomers were right in their calculations, to survey it and take back the word. And after that, Jason wondered, what would happen? Would the humans rest with having satisfied an intellectual curiosity, or would they reassert their ancient ownership—although he doubted very much that at any time man could have been said to have truly owned the Earth. Rather, they had taken it, wresting it from the other creatures that had as much right of ownership as they, but without the intelligence or the ingenuity or power to assert their rights. Man had been the pushy, arrogant interloper rather than the owner. He had taken over by the force of mind, which could be as detestable as the force of muscle, making his own rules, setting his own goals, establishing his own values in utter disregard of all other living things.

A shadow lifted out of a grove of oaks and sailed down into a deep ravine, to be swallowed by the shadow and the silence of which it was a part. An owl, Jason told himself. There were a lot of them, but no one but a night-roamer ever had a chance to see them, for they hid themselves by day. Something ran rustling through the leaves and Bowser cocked an ear at it and snuffled, but either knew too much or was too old and stiff to attempt a chase. A weasel more than likely, or possibly a mink, although this was a bit too far from water for a mink. Too big for a mouse, too silent for a rabbit or an otter.

A man got to know his neighbors, Jason told himself, when he no longer hunted them. In the old days he hunted them, and so had many of the others once the wildlife had been given the chance to grow back to numbers that made hunting reasonable. Sport, they called it, but that had been nothing more than a softer name for the bloodlust that man had carried with him from prehistoric days, when hunting had been a business of keeping life intact—man blood brother to the other carnivores. And man, he thought, the greatest carnivore of all. Now there was no need for such as he to prey upon his brothers of the woodland and the marsh. Meat was supplied by the herds and flocks, although even so he supposed that even this equated to a modified carnivorous mode of life. Even if one wanted to hunt he would have had to revert to the bow and arrow and the lance. The guns still rested in their cases and were meticulously cleaned and oiled by robotic hands, but the supply of powder long had been exhausted and no way, without much study and laborious effort, that it could be resupplied.

The path bent up the hill to the little field where the corn stood in scattered shocks, the pumpkins still upon the ground. In another day or two the robots would haul in the pumpkins for storage, but the corn probably would be left in the shocks until all the other work of autumn had been done. It could be brought in later or, more likely, shucked in the field even after snow lay upon the ground.

In the dim moonlight, the shocks reminded Jason of an Indian encampment and the sight made him wonder if the robots had taken down to Horace Red Cloud's camp the flour and corn meal, the bacon and all the other supplies that he had ordered taken. The chances were they had. The robots were most meticulous in all matters and he fell to wondering, as he had many times before, exactly what they got out of such an arrangement as caring for him and Martha, the house and farm. Or, for that matter, what any robot got out of anything at all . . . Hezekiah and the others in the monastery, the robots at their mysterious building project up the river. This wonderment, he realized, grew out of the old profit motive which had been the obsession and the mainstay of the ancient human race. You didn't do a thing unless there was some material return. Which, of course, was wrong, but the old habit, the old way of thinking, sometimes still intruded and he felt a touch of shame that it should still intrude.

If the humans should repossess the Earth, the old profit motive and the subsidiary philosophies that depended on it would be reestablished, and the Earth, except for whatever benefits it might have gained from its five thousand years of rest from the human plague, would be no better off than it had been before. There was just a bare possibility, he knew, that there would be no move to repossess it. They would know, of course, that the bulk of its resources had been depleted, but even that consideration might not be taken into account. There might be (he could not be sure and John had said nothing about it) a yearning in many of them to return to the ancestral planet. Five thousand years should be a long enough span of time to make the planets on which they now resided seem like home, but one could not be certain. At the very best, Earth would be subjected, more than likely, to streams of tourists and of pilgrims coming back to pay sentimental homage to mankind's parent planet.

He passed the cornfield and went along a narrow

ridge to the point of rocks that hung above the meeting of the rivers. The waning moon made the converging streams shining silver roads cutting through the dark woodlands of the valley. He sat down on the boulder where he always sat, wrapping his heavy cape around him against the chill night wind. Sitting in the silence and hushed loneliness, he was surprised to find himself untouched by the loneliness. For this was home, he thought, and no man could be lonely who stayed close within his home.

That was why, of course, he viewed with such horror the arrival of the People. He could not abide the invasion of his home, of the land that he had made his territory as truly as other animals marked out their territorial rights—not by virtue, however, of any human right, not through any sense of ownership, but by the quiet procedure of simply living here. Not taking over, not contending with his little wildlife neighbors the right to use and walk the land, but by simply staying on in very simple peace.

It could not be allowed, he told himself. They could not be allowed to come back and spoil the Earth again. They could not, for a second time, contaminate it with their machines. He must find a way to stop them, and even as he thought that he must find a way, he knew there was no way. One old and selfish man could not stand against all humanity; perhaps he had no right to stand against humanity. They had their three planets only, and the Earth would make a fourth, while the other small segment of humanity, those not taken in the net that had swept the others off the Earth, had all the galaxy, all the universe, perhaps, if the time ever came when they wished to spread throughout the universe.

Except that he'd not gone out into the galaxy, neither he nor Martha. This was their home, not just these few acres, but the entire Earth. And there was, as well, the others—the Leech Lake Indians. What of them? What would happen to them and their way of life if the others should come back? Another reservation? Another penning up?

Back on the ridge a stone was dislodged by something and went rolling down the slope. Jason sprang swiftly to his feet.

"Who's out there?" he demanded.

It might be a bear. It might be a deer. It was neither.

"It's Hezekiah, sir," a voice said. "I saw you leave the house and I followed you."

"Come on in," said Jason. "Why did you follow me?"

"To give you thanks," the robot said. "My very heartfelt thanks."

He came lumbering out of the darkness.

"Sit down," said Jason. "That boulder over there. It is comfortable."

"I have no need of comfort. I have no need to sit."

"And yet you do," said Jason. "I see you often sitting on the bench beneath the willow tree."

"It is an affectation only," Hezekiah said. "An aping of my betters and a quite unworthy act. I feel great shame of it."

"Continue in your shame," said Jason, "if you enjoy it, but please humor me. I have a need of comfort and a need to sit and shall feel most uncomfortable if you continue standing."

"If you insist," said Hezekiah.

"Indeed I do," said Jason, "and now what is this imaginary kindness for which you wish to thank me?"

"It concerns the pilgrim."

"Yes, I know. Thatcher told me of him."

"I am fairly certain," the robot said, "that he is not a pilgrim. Nicodemus, I know, told Thatcher that he was. Nicodemus got carried away. It is so easy, sir, to get carried away when you want something very much."

"I can understand," said Jason.

"It would have been so wonderful if he had been

a pilgrim. It would have meant that the word had
spread of the labor in which we are engaged. Not
a robot pilgrim, you understand, but a human pilgrim . . ."

Jason sat quietly. The wind fluttered the robe that
the robot wore. Hezekiah picked at it, trying to wrap
it more closely about himself.

"Pride," he said. "That's the thing to fight. Like
sitting down when there is no need to sit. Wearing a
robe when there is need of none. Pacing up and
down the garden, thinking, when one could think as
well if one were standing still."

Jason sat unmoving, keeping his mouth tight shut
when he wanted to scream questions: What about
this pilgrim? Who is he? Where did he come from?
What has he been doing all these years? But remembering with a sour amusement that up until a few
moments ago the worry and the fret of the human
race returning had blanketed out any real concern
about the stranger at the monastery.

"The thing I want to say is this," said Hezekiah.
"I know how long the humans at the House hunted
for other humans in the world. I recall all the rumors
that were brought and how, rumor by rumor, you
were disappointed. Now a human does show up and
you'd have been quite within your rights to have
come hurrying down to claim him. And yet you did
not do it. You stayed away. You let us have our
human. You gave us our hour of glory."

"We figured that it was your show," said Jason.
"We talked about it and decided to stay away. We
can talk with this man later. There is little likelihood
that he will run off. He must have traveled far to
get here."

"Our hour of glory," Hezekiah said, "and an
empty hour, for we know now we did no more than
delude ourselves. I sometimes wonder if our whole
life may not be delusion."

"You'll not get me," said Jason, "to wallow on

the ground with you in your game of martyr. You've sat down there for years, I know, and eaten out your hearts, wondering if you were doing right, if you might be engaged in blasphemy, if you should not be stricken dead for your presumption. Well, the answer is that you've not been stricken dead . . ."

"You mean that you approve. That you, a human . . ."

"No," said Jason. "Not approve, or disapprove. What basis do I have to judge?"

"But once upon a time . . ."

"Yes, I know. Once upon a time man made images out of sticks and clay and worshiped them. Once upon a time he thought the sun was God. How many times must man be mistaken before he learns the truth?"

"I see your point," said Hezekiah. "Do you think we may ever know the truth?"

"How much do you want to know the truth?"

"We seek it," said Hezekiah, "with all our energies. That's the purpose in us, is it not?"

"I don't know," said Jason. "I wish very much I did."

He thought how ridiculous it was, sitting on this windy ridge in the dead of night, talking about the possibility of truth—of any truth, at all—with a fanatic robot. He could tell Hezekiah about the Principle that John had found. He could tell him about the alien who had come to seek a soul. And what good would it do if he told him either?

"I tell you my troubles," Hezekiah said. "You have troubles of your own. You walk the night thinking of your trouble."

Jason grunted uncommittally. He might have suspected. The robots knew what was going on, sometimes, it seemed, before you knew of it yourself. They walked quietly when they wished and heard and, once heard, the news sprang from one to the other of them like an electric impulse. Thatcher would have heard the talk at dinner and later on the patio while they listened to the concert, with the evening clean and beautiful after the passing of the rain (and, come to think of it, there had been something very funny happened at the concert). But it was not only Thatcher. Thatcher, perhaps, less than all the rest of them. They always were around. They listened and they pried and later they talked it over interminably among themselves. There was nothing wrong in it, of course. There was nothing that one had any wish to hide. But their obsession with every little detail of the human world sometimes was disconcerting.

"I," said Hezekiah, "share your great concern."

"How is that?" Jason asked, surprised.

"I understand how you must feel," the robot told him. "Perhaps not all the others, out among the stars. But you and Miss Martha, certainly the two of you . . ."

"Not only us," said Jason. "How about the tribes? The lives of their ancestors were dislocated once. Must it happen again? They have made a new life for themselves. Must they give it up? And how about your people? Would you be happier if there were more humans? At times I think you would."

"Some of us, perhaps," said Hezekiah. "Our function is to serve and there are so few to serve. If only the tribes . . ."

"But you know they won't. They'll have none of you."

"I was about to say," said Hezekiah, "that there is a certain segment of us who might not look kindly upon their coming back. I do not know too much about them, but they are engaged upon a project . . ."

"You mean the installation up the river?"

The robot nodded. "You might talk with them. You might find some help."

"You think that they would help us, would be willing to?"

"There is talk," said Hezekiah, "of marvelous new ideas, of very cunning work. There is none of it I can understand."

Jason sat hunched upon his boulder. He shivered and drew the cape close about his shoulders. The night suddenly seemed darker and lonely and perhaps a little frightening.

"Thank you," he said. "I'll see about it."

In the morning he'd go down to the river landing and talk with Horace Red Cloud. Horace might know what could be done.

14

(Excerpt from journal of Sept. 18, 2185) . . .
Sometime after we had started our ambitious expeditions to get together a comprehensive library and to acquire at least a sampling of the arts, four robots came to see me. I did not recognize them—after all, there are few distinguishing marks by which a robot can be recognized. They may have been working about the farm for years or they may just then have wandered in. I am somewhat surprised, now that I write of it, that I did not question them more closely, but my best memory now is that I did not ask them about their origins, either then or since. It may have been that I was so astonished—and in a sense, upset —by what they had to ask that I was delinquent in my investigation of them.

They told me that their names were Hezekiah, Nicodemus, Jonathon and Ebenezer, and that if I had no objection they would like to occupy the monastery buildings down the road and devote their entire time to a study of Christianity. They seemed to have gotten the idea that man had stopped far short of the point he should have reached in his study of religion and that they, as objective students, might press the matter much beyond man's short-range venture into it. I could detect about them no sign of religious fervor, although I greatly fear that if they continue at it (they have been at it, at the time of this writing, almost thirty years) they will not be able to maintain an objective attitude and may develop unthinking religious fanaticism. I am not even now convinced (perhaps now less convinced than I was then) that I was right in raising no objections to their project. It may not have been right or wise to turn a group of robots loose upon so sensitive a subject. I suppose fanatics have their proper niche in all societies, but the thought of fanatic robots (fanatic on any subject, and religion somehow seems to breed fanatics) does not particularly enchant me. The entire business suggests a situation that can be really frightening. With the most of mankind gone and all the robots left, the robots in time may move to fill the vacuum thus created. They were made to serve us and they cannot, by the very nature of them, be idle. One wonders if, lacking men to serve, in time they will not somehow contrive to serve themselves. If that should be the case, what sort of motives might they have and what kind of purpose? Surely not human and for that, I would suppose, one might be duly grateful. But it is with what I tell myself is pardonable apprehension that one must view the rise of a new philosophy and a setting of new values by creatures that were created in their final form little more than a century ago, having no evolutionary period in which they could develop by the same slow process as man and the other creatures of the Earth (not forgetting that man, even with his long history, may have developed far too fast). It may be that they will take time to evolve, not consciously, of course, but because they will need the time to form, for themselves, a logical operating base. But the time will be short, I fear, and because of this the possibility of serious flaws exists. Evolution supplies the time for testing and rejecting and because of this, has a way of straightening out the kinks in a way of life. For the robots there can be little in the way of evolution and thus many of the kinks will be carried over into their final thinking.

But I get beyond my story. To get back to the four who came to see me. If they were to carry on the work that they proposed, they said, they must have a large body of religious writings and they wondered if they could go along with us on our book-hunting expeditions, being willing to help us with the labor in return for our hauling back the books selected for their studies. The offer of labor was much beside the point, for we had all the robots that we needed for the actual work. But for some reason which I now do not understand (and may not have understood at the time) I agreed. Perhaps the agreement came because the thing they proposed to do seemed more ridiculous than it does now. I may even have chuckled at it then, although after further deliberations I have no chuckles for it.

The collection of our library proved a much harder task than I had anticipated. It was an easy matter, on the face of it, to sit down and write a list, saying that we need Shakespeare, Proust, Plato, Aristotle, Virgil, Gibbon, Locke, Euripides, Aristophanes, Tolstoy, Pascal, Chaucer, Montaigne, Hemingway, Wolfe, Steinbeck, Faulkner and all the others that would go on any list; that we needed texts on mathematics, engineering, chemistry, astronomy, biology, philosophy, psychology and many other branches of the arts and sciences, with the possible exception of medicine, which no longer seems necessary to those of us on Earth (although one can't be entirely sure of that), but how can one be sure he has not missed something that at sometime in the future will be, not sadly missed, for not knowing of it, it will not be missed, but which will not be there for use when there could be need of it. And how does one, obversely, know that much of what he does select may not, in time to come, be unworthy of the space it takes?

Over the years, of course, there may be opportunity to supply any deficit, to obtain what might have been overlooked. But as the years go on, it will be more difficult to do. Even when we collected the books we had great difficulties. The trucks we used required continual tinkering to keep them running and in many cases the roads had deteriorated, through flood and frost and other circumstances, to a point where they were often hard to travel. At some places, we were forced to make detours. The trucks, of course, are no longer usable; after a time even the most determined tinkering could not keep them running. The roads, I would presume, are now much farther góne to ruin, although they still possibly could be used by wagons. I can foresee a time (although we tried our best to guard against such an eventuality) when mēn, seeking a particular book or books, of which they might have found some reference, will be forced to strike out afoot or by pack train through the wilderness in hopes of finding a still existent library or some other depository where there still may exist the books we may have forgotten to place upon our list.

By that time, perhaps, the books no longer will exist. Even housed under the best circumstances in the long deserted cities, the weather will get at them, and the rodents and the worms, and if nothing else, sheer time will take the toll.

We finally located and transported here all the books that we had listed. With the art objects we sought to salvage we encountered greater problems, principally because with them space was a greater consideration than it is with books. We had to painfully select and choose with the greatest care. How many Rembrandts, for example, could we allow ourselves, knowing that each éxtra Rembrandt would rob us of a Courbet or a Renoir? Because of the very lack of space, both in transportation and in storage, we were forced to choose the smaller canvas rather than the larger. The same criterion applied to all other categories of the arts.

There are times when I could weep, thinking of all the great endeavors and accomplishments of mankind we were forced to leave to be forever lost . . .

15

Horace Red Cloud squatted by the fire for a long time after the two white men had left. He had watched them leave, going up the hollow that ran back into the hills, until a twisting of the hollow had hidden them from view, and after they were gone, had stayed by the fire, unmoving. The morning was far gone, but as yet the camp lay in shadow, the sun not having risen enough into the sky to clear the towering bluffs that blocked its light. The camp was quiet, quieter than usual—the others knew something was afoot, but they would not intrude upon him, there beside the fire; they would not ask, but wait for him to tell them. The women went about their work as usual, but with less commotion, without a banging of the pans and yelling back and forth. The small-fry huddled, quiet in groups, whispering to one another, bursting with excitement. The others were not in camp—perhaps working in the cornfields, although some of them would be fishing or out prowling. One could not expect a man, especially a young man, to spend an entire day at drudgery. Even the dogs were quiet.

The fire had burned to a gray ash, with some blackened sticks showing at its edges and a hint of heat lying in its heart, with only the smallest trickle of smoke rising from the ash and the ends of the blackened sticks. Slowly he put out his hands, holding them in the smoke, scrubbing them together, washing them with smoke. He did it absentmindedly and was somewhat amused when he saw what he was doing. A cultural reflex action, he wondered, still keeping his hands where they were, still washing them with smoke. Thus his far ancestors had washed their hands in smoke as a purification rite, one of the many senseless little gestures they went through when they stood upon the brink of magic, symbolically purifying themselves so they could deal in magic. And how much had he and the others lost when they had turned their backs on magic? Belief, of course, and there might be some value in belief, although there was, as well, delusion and did a man want to pay for the value of belief in the coinage of delusion? Although we've lost very little, he told himself, and have gained a great deal more—an understanding of ourselves as a factor of ecology. We have learned to live with trees and water, with earth and sky and wind, with weather, and the wild things, as if they were brothers to us. Using them as we need them, not abusing our need and use of them, respecting them, living with them, being one with them. Not using them as the white man did, not owning them, not ignoring them, with no contempt of them.

He got up slowly from the fire and went down the path toward the river. Where the path ended at the water's edge canoes were drawn up on the gravel beach and a yellowed willow tree, its branches drooping, dipped the gold of its leaves into the flowing stream. Upon the water were other floating leaves, the red and brown of oak, the scarlet of the maple, the yellow of the elm—the tributes of other trees farther up the stream, their offerings to the river that had supplied the water that they needed through the hot, dry days of summer. The river talked to him, not to him alone, he knew, but to the trees, the hills, the sky, a friendly mumbling gossip that ran down across the land.

He stooped and cupped his hands together, plunged them in the river and then lifted them. His hands were full, but the water ran between his fingers and escaped, leaving a little puddle of it where the edges of his palms were pressed together. He opened the hands and let the water go, back into the river. That was the way it should be, he told himself. The water and the air and earth ran away when you tried to grasp them. They would not be caught and held. They were not something one could own, but something one could live with. It had been so long ago in the first beginning, and then there had been men who had tried to own them, to hold them, to influence and coerce them, and after that there had been a new beginning and was that new beginning to come to an end again?

I shall call all the tribes together, he had told Jason, sitting at the fire. It is near the time to make the winter meat, but this is more important than the winter meat. It had, perhaps, been silly for him to say a thing like that, for he should have known— and did know—that a throng a thousand times as large as all the tribes would not prevail against the whites if they wanted to come back. Strength was not enough, determination would be futile, love of homeland and devotion to it stood as nothing against men who could cross between the stars on ships. They took one path, he thought, and we took another, from the very first and ours was not the wrong path (indeed, it was the right one), but it made us weak against their rapacity, as everything was weak against their rapacity.

These had been good years since they had gone away. There had been time to find the old paths once again. Once again the wind blew free and the water ran untrammeled down the land. Once more the prairie grass grew thick and sweet and the forest was a forest once again and the sky was black in spring and fall with wildfowl.

He did not like the idea of visiting the robot installation, he recoiled against the robot, Hezekiah, riding in a canoe, sharing even temporarily this ancient way of life, but Jason was quite right—it was the only thing to do, it was the only chance they had.

He turned back up the path, toward the camp. They all were waiting and now he'd call them all together. The men would be picked to paddle canoes. Some of the young men would have to secure fresh meat and fish for the journey. The women must get together food and robes. There was much to do; they'd set out in the morning.

16

Evening Sar was sitting on the patio when the young man with the binoculars and the bear-claw necklace showed up, coming up the path from the monastery.

He stopped in front of her. "You are here to read the books," he said. "That is the correct word, is it not? To read?"

He wore a white bandage on his cheek. "You have the word," she said. "Won't you please sit down. How are you feeling?"

"Very well," he said. "The robots took good care of me."

"Well, then, sit down," she said. "Or are you going somewhere?"

"I have nowhere to go," he said. "I may go no farther." He sat down in a chair beside her and laid the bow upon the flagstones. "I had wanted to ask you about the trees that make the music. You know about the trees. Yesterday you spoke with the ancient oak . . ."

"You told me," she said, somewhat angrily, "that you'd never mention that again. You spied upon me and you promised."

"I am sorry, but I must," he told her. "I have never met a person who could talk with trees. I have never heard before a tree that could make music."

"What have the two to do with one another?"

"There was something wrong with the trees last night. I thought perhaps you noticed. I think I did something to them."

"You must be joking. Who could do anything with the trees? And there was nothing wrong with them. They played beautifully."

"There was a sickness in them, or in some of them. They played not as well as they could play. And I did something with the bears as well. Especially that last bear. Maybe with all of them."

"You told me that you killed them. And took one claw from each to put into the necklace. A way of keeping count, you said. And, if you ask me, a way of bragging, too."

She thought he might get angry, but he only looked a little puzzled. "I had thought all the time," he said, "that it was the bow. That I killed them because I could shoot the bow so well and the arrows were so finely fashioned. What if it were not the bow at all, or the arrows or my shooting of them, but something else entirely?"

"What difference does it make? You killed them, didn't you?"

"Yes, of course I killed them, but . . ."

"My name is Evening Star," she said, "and you've never told me yours."

"I am David Hunt."

"And so, David Hunt, tell me about yourself."

"There is not much to tell."

"But there must be something. You have people and a home. You surely came from somewhere."

"A home. Yes, I suppose so. Although we moved around a lot. We were always fleeing and the people leaving . . ."

"Fleeing? What was there to flee from?"

"The Dark Walker. I see you do not know of it. You have not heard of it?"

She shook her head.

"A shape," he said. "Like a man and yet not like a man. Two-legged. Maybe that is the only way it is like a man. Never seen in daytime. Always seen at night. Always on a ridgetop, black against the sky. It was first seen on the night everyone was taken— that is, everyone but us, and I suppose, to say it right, everyone but us and the people here and those out on the plains. I am the first of our people to know there are other people."

"You seem to think there is only one Dark Walker. Are you sure of that? Are you sure there really is a Dark Walker, or do you just imagine it? My people at one time imagined so many things that we now know were never true. Has it ever hurt any of your people?"

He frowned, trying to think. "No, not that I know of. It hurt no one; it is only seen. It is horrible to see. We watch for it all the time and when we see it, we flee to somewhere else."

"You never tried to track it down?"

"No," he said.

"I thought perhaps that was what you were doing now. Trying to track it down and kill it. A great bowman such as you, who can kill the bears . . ."

"You make fun of me," he said, but without a show of anger.

"Perhaps," she said. "You are so proud of the killing of the bears. No one of my people have killed so many bears."

"I doubt," he said, "that the Walker could be killed with arrows. Maybe it can not be killed at all."

"There may be no Walker," said the girl. "Have you ever thought of that? Surely, if there were, we would have seen or heard of it. My people range far west to the mountains and there'd have been some word of it. And so far as that goes, how is it that all these years there has been no word of your people? For centuries the people in this house hunted other people, running down all sorts of rumors."

"So did my people, I am told, in the early years. I have only heard of it, of course. Things that people talked about. I have, myself, only twenty summers."

"We are the same age," said Evening Star. "I am just nineteen."

"There are few young people among us," said David Hunt. "There are not many of us, all of us together, and we move around so much . . ."

"It puzzles me," she said, "that there are only a few of you. If you are like the rest of us, you live for a long, long time and there is no sickness. From one small tribe, my people number many thousands. From a few people in this house there are thousands in the stars. There should be thousands of you. You should be strong and many . . ."

"We could be many," he said, "but we go away."

"I thought you told me . . ."

"Not to the stars, like these others. But across the water. There is a madness that sends many of us across the water. They build rafts and they set out across the water, toward the setting sun. It has been done for many years. I don't know why. I never have been told."

"Perhaps fleeing from the Walker."

"I don't think so," he said. "I don't think those who go know why they are going or even that they're going until the madness seizes them."

"Lemmings," said Evening Star.

"What are lemmings?"

"Small animals. Rodents. I read about them once."

"What have lemmings to do with us?"

"I am not sure," she said.

"I ran away," he said. "Myself and Old Jose. We both feared the bigness of the water. We did not want to go if the few remaining people went. If we ran away, we said, the madness might not touch us. Jose saw the Walker, twice, after we had run away, and we ran again, from the Walker, very far and fast."

"When Jose saw the Walker, did you . . ."

"No. I've never seen it."

"Do you think the other people went? Out across the water, after you and Jose left?"

"I do not know," he said. "Jose died. He was an old, old man. He remembered when the People disappeared. He was an old man even then. There came a day when his life ran out. I think that he was glad. It is not always good to live too long. When you live too long you too often are alone."

"But he had you with him."

"Yes, but there were too many years between us. We got along all right and we talked a lot, but he missed the people like himself. He would play the fiddle and I would listen and the coyotes would sit up on the hills and sing with the fiddle. Have you ever heard a coyote sing?"

"I've heard them bark and howl," she said. "I never heard one sing."

"They sang every night when Old Jose would play. He'd play only in the evening. There were a lot of coyotes and I think they came to listen and to sing along. There were times when there'd be a dozen of them, sitting on the hilltops, singing. Jose said he couldn't play as well as he should. His fingers were no longer limber and his arm was heavy with the bow. I felt the death that was in him, death sitting on the hilltop and listening with the wolves. When he died I dug a deep hole and buried him, with the fiddle beside him, for it was no use to me and I thought he'd like it that way. Then I worked for days, carrying rocks, as big as I could pack, to pile upon the grave against the wolves. All the time I did this I was not lonesome, for somehow it seemed that I was still with Jose. Working for him was like being with him. But once I finished, I was lonely."

"You could have gone back to find your people."

"I thought of it," he said, "but I had no idea where they were and I still was afraid of the madness that might send me out with them upon the water. I had a feeling that the madness would not strike me if I were alone. It is—what would you call it?—a group madness. And, besides, there was something inside of me that kept telling me to go toward the rising sun. I have wondered many times what it was that made me go. There seemed no reason that I should. It was as if I were hunting for something, although I did not know what it is I am supposed to hunt. I found your people out on the plains and I wanted to stay with them. They would have let me stay. But I couldn't. The call of the rising sun still was in me and I had to leave them. They told me of this great stone house and I wondered if that was what I had set out to find. There were many houses of stone that I found along the way, but I was afraid of them. My people never lived in houses. We were afraid of them. They made noises in the night and they were so empty and we thought that there were ghosts in them, maybe the ghosts of the people who had been taken when everyone disappeared."

"You're here now," said the girl. "I hope you stay awhile. You'll find nothing to the east. It is only empty forest. A few of my people live there, but even so, it all is empty forest. And this house is not like the houses that you saw. It is not empty; it is lived in. It has the feel of people."

"The robots would let me stay with them," he said. "They are kindly folks."

"But," she said, "they aren't human. You'll want to be with humans. Uncle Jason and Aunt Martha, I am sure, would be glad to have you. Or, if you'd rather, there always would be a place for you in my people's camp."

"Uncle Jason and Aunt Martha live in this house?"

"Yes, but they really aren't aunt and uncle to me.

I call them that, but only to myself. They do not
know I call them that. Uncle Jason and my
grandfather-many-times-removed have been lifelong
friends. They were young men at the Disappearance."

"I may have to go on," he said. "The call of the
rising sun may not have left me yet. But I'd be glad
of a little time to rest. I came to ask you about your
talking with the trees. You have not told me of it.
Do you talk with all the trees, or just a certain tree?"

"You may not understand," she said. "We live
close to the trees, the streams, the flowers, the animals and birds. We are one with them. Any one of
us can talk with them."

"And you the best of all."

"I would not know. Among ourselves we do not
discuss it. I can speak only for myself. I can go for
a walk, into the woods or along a stream, and I am
never lonely or alone, for I meet so many friends and
I always talk with them."

"And they talk back to you."

"Sometimes they do," she said.

"You talk with the trees and the others go out to
the stars."

"You still don't believe about the stars."

"I am beginning to," he said. "Although it is hard
to believe it. I asked the robots about it and they
explained it to me, although I do not think I understood entirely. They said that of all the people once
in this house, only two remain. The rest are out
among the stars. They said that at times they come
back from the stars for a visit. Is that so?"

"Yes, it is. There is one of them now back from
the stars. Uncle Jason's brother. He brought disturbing word. He and Uncle Jason went down to the
camp this morning to talk with my many-times-grand-
father about the word he brought."

She was running on too much, she thought. Perhaps Uncle Jason would not like her telling this to a
perfect stranger, a man who had stumbled out of

nowhere. It had just slipped out, as if he were a friend. And she did not really know him. She had met him only yesterday after he had spied on her and again this morning when he'd come up the road from the monastery. But it was, she thought, as if she'd known him for years. He was just a boy. What was it he had said about the many years that lay between himself and his old friend? Maybe that was it. There were no years to lie between the two of them.

"You think," he asked, "that your aunt and uncle would not mind my staying here? You could ask your aunt, perhaps."

"Not now," said Evening Star. "She is talking with the stars. She has been talking all the morning. But we can ask her later—or my uncle when he returns from camp."

17

He felt old and lonely. It was the first time in years that he had felt lonely and the first time ever that he'd had a sense of being old.

"I debated telling you," said Martha. "Perhaps I should not have told you, Jason, but you had to know. They were all polite and understanding . . ."

"And a bit amused," he said.

"I don't think quite that," she told him. "But a little baffled as to why you should be so upset. Earth can't mean as much to them, of course, as it means to you and me. Some of them have never been here. To them Earth is only an old and beautiful story. And all of them pointed out that the others may have no intention of coming back and staying; it might simply be an exploratory trip to satisfy their curiosity."

"The point is," said Jason, "that they don't really care. They have the stars; they don't need Earth. As you say, it's just a story to them. I had thought of calling a conference—some of the old and trusted friends, some of the younger ones to whom we've been the closest."

"It still might be a good idea," Martha said. "They would come, I'm sure. All of them would come, I think, if we really needed them. It might do a lot of good. There are so many things that they have learned. We don't know of all the things they've learned."

"I wouldn't count too much on what they've learned," said John. "Collectively, they have learned a great deal. Since they've gone to the stars the sum total of the knowledge they have gained probably is as great or greater than all that man had learned on Earth before the Disappearance. But this knowledge is superficial. They have learned the surface facts, that a certain thing is possible or that certain action will bring about a prescribed effect, but they've gained no real understanding for they have not sought the why and wherefore of it. And because of this, while they know many strange and unguessed things, the knowledge does them little good, for they cannot use it. And a lot of it, as well, is defiant of any human understanding. Much of it is so alien to the human concept of the universe that it can't be understood until a man has mastered alien viewpoints and intellectual processes and . . ."

"You need not go on," said Jason, bitterly. "I know how impossible it is."

"I've not wanted to point this out," said John, "because I know you will not like it. But, if worse comes to worst, you and Martha can go to the stars."

"John, you know I can't do that," said Jason. "And I don't think Martha could. Earth is in our bones. We've lived with it too long. It's too much a part of us."

"I've often wondered what it would be like," said Martha. "I've talked to so many people and they've told me so much of it. But if it came to going, I don't think I could go."

"You see," said Jason, "we're just two old selfish people."

And that's the truth of it, he told himself. It's a selfish thing to hang onto Earth, to claim it, all of it, for one's own. When one came right down to it, the People had a right to return to Earth if that should be their wish. They'd not left Earth of their own free will; they had been abducted from it; they had been taken from it. If they could find their way back to it, there was no legal and no moral stricture barring their return. The worst thing about it all, he realized, would be their insistence on sharing with those still left on Earth all that they had learned and gained, all their technological advances, all their bright new concepts, all their shimmering knowledge, determined to give free-handedly to the benighted people left on Earth all the advantages of the continuing human heritage. And what of the tribes, who wanted none of this? And the robots, too? Although maybe the robots would welcome their return. He knew little of the robots or how they might feel about such a circumstance.

In a day or two he'd know how the robots felt about it. Tomorrow morning he and John and Hezekiah would set out up the river with Red Cloud and his men.

18

(Excerpt from journal of Oct. 9, 3935) . . . I have hesitated to accept the business of going to the stars. I knew it was being done; I knew it was possible; I saw them go and, after a time, return. And I talked with them about it; all of us have talked about it at great length and, being human, have sought to determine the mechanism that makes it possible and even at times, although less often now, have debated the desirability of this trait we discovered. And the use of that word, trait, is most revealing, for it lends emphasis to the fact that we know nothing whatever about how we do it or how it might have come about.

I say there has been some hesitancy on my part to accept going to the stars and that is, I know, a somewhat confusing statement and I am not sure at all that I can make it clear. I, of course, have accepted it intellectually and even emotionally in that I have been as excited about this seeming impossibility as have any of the others. But the acceptance is not total. It is as if I were shown some impossible animal or plant (impossible for any number of good and logical reasons). Seeing it, I would be forced to admit that it did, indeed, exist. But turning and walking away from it, I'd find myself doubting the evidence of my eyes and telling myself that I had not actually seen it, in consequence of which I'd have to go back and see it once again. And when I turned away from it the second time, and the third and fourth and fifth, I'd still find myself doubtful of what I had seen and have to turn back to reassure myself. Perhaps there is something more as well. Try as I may, I cannot make up my mind that this is a beneficial, or even a proper, thing for any human being to do. A built-in caution, perhaps, or a resistance to anything too revolutionary (an attitude not uncommon in one of my biological age) niggles at me continually, whispering warnings of catastrophe as a result of this new ability. The conservatism in me will not accept that so great a thing can be conferred upon the human race without the exaction of some sort of heavy payment. Feeling so, I suppose that unconsciously I have gone on the assumption that until I unreservedly admit that it is so, it cannot be so and that until it actually becomes so, the payment can be deferred.

All of this, of course, is egocentric and, more than that, plain foolish and I have felt at times, although everyone has been at great pains not to make it so appear, that I have made a great fool of myself. For the trips to the stars have been going on for some years now and by this time almost everyone has gone for at least one short trip. I have not gone, of course; my doubts and reservations no doubt would act as a psychological block to my going, which is something that is idle to speculate upon, for I don't intend to try. My grandson Jason and his excellent Martha are among the few who have not gone and my prejudice makes me very glad of this. I seem to see in Jason some of the same love of the ancestral acres that I have myself and I am inclined to believe that this love will keep him forever from the stars which, mistaken though I may be, I account no tragedy. His brother, John, however, was among the first to go and he has not come back. I have spent many hours of worry over him.

It is ridiculous, of course, for me to persist in this illogical attitude. Whatever I may say or think, man finally has severed, quite naturally and as a matter of course, his dependence on the Earth. And that may be the core of how I feel about it—an uneasiness that Man should, after long millennia, finally end his dependence on the Earth.

The house is filled with mementos from the stars. Amanda just this morning brought the beautiful bouquet of most strange flowers that sits upon my desk, plucked on a planet of which I now quite forget the name—although the name is not important, for it is not really its name (if it ever had a name) but a name by which two human beings, Amanda and her boyfriend, George, have designated it. It is out toward a bright star of which I now also forget the name—not a planet of that particular star, of course, but of a smaller neighbor, so much fainter that even if we had a large telescope we could not pick up its light. All about the house are strange objects—branches with dried berries, colorful rocks and pebbles, chunks of exotic wood, fantastic artifacts picked from sites where intelligent creatures once had lived and built and fabricated the cultural debris that we now bring back. We have no photographs and that's a pity, for while we have the cameras, still in working condition, we have no film to load them with. Some day someone may develop a way of making film again and we'll have photographs. Strangely, I am the only one who has considered photographs; none of the others have any interest in them.

At first there was a fear that someone, returning from the stars, would coalesce, or otherwise come back together in their natural form, at the exact location of some solid object or, perhaps, another person, which in the last instance, would be extremely messy. I don't think there was ever any real need for apprehension, for as I understand it, the returning traveler, before he aims for his next point of materialization, peeps or scans or otherwise becomes aware of the situation and condition of the location he is aiming at. I must admit that I am very bad at writing this, for despite being associated with it for a number of years, I do not understand what is going on, which may be due to the fact that the ability which the others have developed has bypassed me entirely.

Anyhow—and this is what I have been leading up to—the large ballroom on the third floor has been set aside as the area in which returning travelers materialize, with the area barred to all others and a rule set up that the entire room be kept clear of any object. Some of the younger people called the room the Depot, harking back to those virtually pre-historic days when buses and trains arrived and de-parted from depots, and the name has stuck. There was at first a great deal of hilarity over the name, for to some of the young folks it seemed very humorous. I must admit that I see no particular humor in it, although I can see no real harm in whatever they may call it.

I have pondered the development of the entire business and, despite some of the theories advanced by others who have actually traveled (and therefore assume they know more of it than I), I believe that what we may have here is a normal evolutionary process—at least, that is what I would like to think it is. Man rose from a lowly primate to intelligence, became a toolmaker, a hunter, a farmer, a controller of his environment—he had progressed steadily through the years and the progress most admittedly has not always been for the good, either to himself or others. But the point is that he has progressed and this going to the stars may be only another evolutionary point that marks a further logical pro-gression . . .

19

Jason couldn't go to sleep. He couldn't quit thinking about the Principle. What had started him to thinking on it he did not know, and as an exercise that might shake him loose from it, he tried to backtrack in his mind to the point where he had first begun his speculations, but the area was fogged and he could not get to the beginning of it and the wondering went on.

He should get to sleep, he told himself. Thatcher would wake him early in the morning and with John he'd set off down the path to Horace Red Cloud's camp. He looked forward to traveling up the river, for it would be interesting—it had been a long time since he had gone far from home—but no matter how interesting it might be, it would be a hard day for him and he needed sleep.

He tried counting sheep and tried adding a column of imaginary figures, but the sheep refused to jump and the figures faded off into the nothingness from which he'd summoned them and he was left with the worry and the wonder of the Principle.

If the universe were steady-state, if it had no beginning and would not have an end, if it had always existed and would continue to exist, at what point in this foreverness had the Principle come into being—or was it, as well as the universe, a foreverness? And if the universe were evolutionary, starting at a certain time and place and destined to come to an end at a certain time and place, had the Principle been there and waiting, a strangeness out of nothingness, or had it evolved only at a later time and from what had it evolved? And why this galaxy, he wondered—why had the Principle chosen to reside within this galaxy, when there were billions of other galaxies that could have been its home? Had it come into being in this galaxy and stayed here, and if that should be the case, what unique characteristics did this galaxy offer to trigger its appearance? Or was it a much larger thing than anyone might imagine, was the manifestation of it in this galaxy only an outpost of a much greater central unity?

It was all absurd, of course. There was no way in which he could find an answer; no means by which he could arrive at even a logical suspicion of what had really happened. He didn't have the data; no one had the data. The only one that would know would be the Principle itself. The whole procedure of his thinking, Jason knew, was an imbecilic exercise; there was no compelling reason for him to seek an answer. And yet his mind bored on and on and he could not stop it, hanging with desperation to an impossibility to which it never should have paid attention.

He turned over restlessly and tried to burrow his head deeper into the pillow.

"Jason," said Martha, out of the darkness, "are you asleep?"

He mumbled to her. "Almost," he said. "Almost."

20

He was polished and he shone in the morning light; he said his name was Stanley and he was glad that they had come. He recognized three of them—Hezekiah, Jason and Red Cloud, in that order—and he said that word and rumor of them had made its way into the Project. Introduced to John, he professed unusual pleasure at meeting a man from among the stars. He was suave and genteel and he glittered when he walked and he said it was neighborly of them to pay a visit, even after all the years, and that he was desolated he could offer neither food nor drink, since robots made no use of either.

Apparently a watch had been kept on them from the time of the flotilla's first appearance, coming up the river, for he had been waiting for them on the blufftop when they came climbing up the path, with the beached canoes and the men who had paddled them waiting on the shore below the bluff.

Above the blufftop towered the structure, whatever it might be—a huge and curving thinness that flared out, with a greater diameter at the top than at that point where it emerged from the ground, black with the shine of many metallic highlights that caught the morning sun, a huge and curving thinness that went up into the sky, more like a fantastic monument or a dreaming sculpture than it was like a structure and, looking at it, it seemed to make no sense. Set in a circle, it did not quite complete the circle, but stood with a V-section of emptiness gaping on one side of it.

From where they stood, at some distance beyond the flaring structure, lay the mounds of the ancient city, with here and there broken walls and the metallic skeletons of buildings still rising above the uneven ground, looking for all the world like the canted arms or the stiffened hands of corpses buried hurriedly and too shallowly for decency.

Across the river stood another mounded area, but here the disintegration of the buildings seemed somewhat less advanced, for at certain intervals great piles of masonry still emerged.

Stanley saw Jason looking at the structures. "The old university," he said. "We have been at great pains to preserve some selected buildings."

"You make use of them?"

"Of the contents of them. Certain instruments and libraries. Old workshops and laboratories. And what was missing in them we have transported, through the years, from other learning centers. Although," he said with a touch of sadness, "there's not much left elsewhere anymore."

"You used the knowledge to build this," said John, indicating the flaring structure with an upward sweep of his arm.

"We did," the robot Stanley said. "You came to hear of it?"

"That, in part," said Jason. "There is something more, however."

"We have a place," said Stanley, "where you can be far more comfortable than standing on this windswept prairie. If you will follow me."

Following him, they went along a beaten path until they came to a ramp that led down into the space enclosed by the flaring structure. As they walked down the ramp, they saw that less than half the structure stood above the ground, that its smooth sides went plunging down into a great hole that had been excavated to accommodate it. The ramp wound steeply downward, curving in a great sweep around the smooth wall of the flaring thing.

"We went down to bedrock to anchor it," said Stanley. "Down to the solid limestone."

"And you call it the Project?" Red Cloud asked. It was the first time he had spoken. Jason had seen him stiffen in something close to outrage when the glittering robot had come out to meet them and had momentarily held his breath, afraid of what his old friend might feel compelled to say. But he had said nothing and Jason had felt for him a surge of affection and admiration. Over the years that Red Cloud had been coming to the house, there had developed between him and Thatcher something that resembled affectionate respect, but Thatcher was the only robot the old chief would give a second glance. And now here was this striding, competent, self-assured dandy of a robot performing as their host. Jason could imagine how the gorge must have risen in the old man's throat at the sight of him.

"That is what we call it, sir," said Stanley. "We called it that to start with and it got to be a habit and we never changed the name. Which is all right, of course. It is the only project that we have."

"And the purpose of it? It must have a purpose?" The way that Red Cloud said it, it was quite apparent he rather doubted that it had.

"Once we get to the place of comfort," the robot said, "I shall tell you all you wish. We have no secrets here."

They met other robots, going up the ramp, but they spoke no greeting and they did not stop. And here, thought Jason, as he went pacing down the ramp, was the explanation of all those hurrying, purposeful bands of so-called "wild robots" they had seen through all the centuries—purposeful, dedicated bands setting off in all directions, and returning from all directions, to get the needed materials for the building of this place.

They finally reached the bottom of the ramp and here the circle of the structure was much smaller than at the top and set in the space at the bottom of the pit was what appeared to be an open-sided house, a roof set on stout columns, housing tables, desks and chairs, along with filing cabinets and some rather strange machines. It was, Jason decided, a combination operations center and construction shack.

"Gentlemen," said Stanley, "if you please will find a place to sit, I shall listen to your questions and endeavor to tell you all you wish. I have associates I can summon . . ."

"One of you is enough," said Red Cloud harshly.

"I think," said Jason, hurrying to cover Red Cloud's words, "we'll not need to bother any of the others. I take it you can answer for the others."

"I have told you," the robot said, "that we have no secrets. And we're all of a single mind, or very nearly so. I can call the others if there is any need. It is not necessary to tell you, I suppose, that I recognized all of you except the gentleman who came from the stars. Your reputations have preceded you. The chief we know and have admired, although we are aware of the animosity that he and his people hold toward us. We can understand the basis of that attitude, although we do regret it, and we have made a point, sir," he said to Red Cloud, "not to intrude ourselves upon you."

"Your tongue," said Red Cloud, "is smoother than it should be, but I grant you have kept out of our way."

"Mr. Jason," said the robot, "we have regarded as a good, great friend and we've been most proud of Hezekiah and the work that he has done."

"If you felt that way," asked Jason, "why did you never come to visit us?"

"We had thought, somehow, that it might not be proper. You may be able to understand a little how we must have felt when suddenly there was no longer men to serve, when the very purpose of our existence was, in a moment, taken from us."

"But others come to us," said Jason. "We are knee-deep in robots, for which we are quite thankful. They have taken splendid care of us."

"That is true," said Stanley, "but you had all you needed. Perhaps far more than you needed. We had no wish to embarrass you."

"Then I would take it," said John, "that you would be glad to hear the People may be coming back."

"The People!" croaked the robot, shaken from the calm of his self-assurance. "The People coming back?"

"They have only been away," said John, "on other planets. They have relocated Earth and a survey ship is on its way. It may be arriving very soon."

Stanley struggled with himself. They could see him struggle. When he finally spoke, he was himself again. "You are sure of this?" he asked.

"Very sure," said John.

"You ask if we would be glad," said Stanley. "I do not think we would."

"But you said . . ."

"That was in the beginning. That was five thousand years ago. In that length of time, there must be changes. You call us machines and I suppose we are. But in five thousand years even a machine can change. Not mechanically, of course. But you made us machines with brains and brains can change. Viewpoints can shift. New values can be arrived at and accepted. Once we worked for men; it was our purpose and our life. Given a choice, we would not have changed the situation. We gained satisfaction from our servitude; we were built to gain satisfaction from a life of servitude. Loyalty was the love we gave the human race and we take no credit for it, for the loyalty was built into us."

"But now," said Hezekiah, "you work for yourself."

"You can understand that, Hezekiah. You and your companions now work for yourselves."

"No," said Hezekiah. "We still work for Man."

The robot Stanley paid no attention to what Hezekiah said. "We were confused at first," he said, "and lost. Not we, of course, but each of us, each one separately. For we had never been one people; there had been no we; just each of us alone, doing what was expected of him, doing what he'd been fabricated for, and happy in the doing of it. We had no life of our own and I think that is what confused us so much when the People went away. For here suddenly, not we, but each of us alone, found that he did have a life of his own, that he could live without his human master, and that he still was capable of functioning had there been anything to do. Many of us stayed on for a time, in some cases a very long time, in the old households, performing the tasks we were supposed to do—as if our people had only gone off on a trip and would soon be coming back. Although even the stupidest of us, I think, knew this was not the case, for not only our own people, but everyone, had gone and that was most peculiar, for never before had everyone gone away at once. I think that the most of us grasped immediately what had happened, but we kept on pretending that it wasn't so, that in time the people would all come home again and, true to our conditioning and training, we continued in the tasks that now were no tasks at all, but simply senseless motions. In time we gave up the pretense, not all of us at once, of course, but a few of us at first and others a little later and others after them. We took to wandering, hunting for new masters, for tasks that were not senseless. We found no humans, but we did find ourselves, we found one another. We talked with one another; we laid our little, short-range, meaningless plans by consultation with others of our kind. First we sought for humans and finally, when we knew there were no humans who would take us in—for your people, Mr. Jason, had all the robots that you needed and your people, Chief Red Cloud, would have none of us, and there was a small band out West, on the coast, who were frightened of everything, even of us who tried to help them . . ."

Red Cloud said to Jason, "That would be the tribe from which your wanderer came. What was it he said they were afraid of? The Dark Walker, wasn't it?"

"They were field workers to begin with," Jason said. "He didn't tell me this, perhaps he doesn't know, but from what he told me it is very plain. Agricultural people who worked continually in the fields, following the plantings, the tending and the harvest. Ground down in poverty, living hand to mouth, tied so close to the soil they became the very soil. They had no robots, of course. They may only have glimpsed robots from a distance, if at all. Even having seen them, they may not have fully understood exactly what they were. The robots were far better off than they. They would have been frightened of a robot."

"They fled from us," said Stanley. "Not from me. I wasn't there. But from others of our people. We tried to make them understand. We tried to explain to them. But still they fled from us. We finally no longer followed them. We had no wish to frighten them."

"What do you think they saw?" asked Red Cloud. "This Dark Walker of theirs . . ."

"Perhaps nothing," Jason said. "They would have had, I suspect, a long background of folklore. They would have been a superstitious people. To people such as they, superstition would have been an entertainment and perhaps a hope . . ."

"But they might have seen something," insisted Red Cloud. "On that night when it happened, there might have been something on the Earth. There may have been netters who swept up the People. In times past my people had their stories of things that walked the Earth and we, in our new sophistication, are too ready to discount them. But when you live as close to the bosom of the Earth as we do you come to realize that some of the old stories may have some shreds of truth in them. We know, for example, that aliens on occasion now do visit Earth and in time past, before the white man came with his fury and his noise, when this continent was quieter and less boisterous than it became, who can say they did not visit then?"

Jason nodded. "Old friend," he said, "you may well be right."

"We came to a time," said the robot Stanley, "when we knew there were no humans we could serve and we stood with idle hands and there was nothing we could do. But through the centuries the idea grew, slowly at first and then with greater impact, that if we could not work for humans, we could work for ourselves. But what can a robot do for himself or for other robots? Build a civilization? A civilization would be meaningless for us. Build a fortune? What would we get a fortune from and what need would we have of it? We had no profit motive, we did not thirst for status. Education we might have been capable of and even have enjoyed, but it was a dead end, for except for a questionable self-satisfaction it might have given us, we had no use for it. Humans used education for their self-improvement, to earn a better living, to contribute to society, to assure themselves of more enjoyment of the arts. They called it self-improvement and that was a worthy goal for any human, but how could a robot improve himself? And to what purpose and what end? The answer seemed to be that we could not improve ourselves. No robot could make himself appreciably better than he already was. He had limitations built into him by his makers. His capabilities were predetermined by the materials and the programming that went into him. Considering the tasks he was designed to do, he served well enough. There was no need for a better robot. But there seemed no doubt that a better robot could be built. Once you thought of it, it became apparent that there was no limit to a robot. There was no place you had to stop and say, this is the best robot we can make. No matter how well a robot was designed, a better one was always possible. What would happen, we asked ourselves, if an open-ended robot should be built, one that was never really finished . . ."

"Are you trying to tell us," Jason asked, "that what you have here is your open-ended robot?"

"Mr. Jason," Stanley said, "that is, indeed, what I have tried to say."

"But what do you intend?"

"We do not know," said Stanley.

"You don't know? You are the ones who are building . . ."

"Not any longer," Stanley said. "It has taken over now. It tells us what to do."

"What use is it?" asked Red Cloud. "It is anchored here. It can't move. It can't do anything."

"It has a purpose," said the robot, stubbornly. "It must have a purpose . . ."

"Now, just a minute there," said Jason. "You say it tells you what to do. You mean that it has taken over the building of itself? That it tells you how to build it?"

Stanley nodded. "It started twenty years or more ago. We have talked with it . . ."

"Talked with it. How?"

"By printout. We talk back and forth, like the old computers."

"What you really have built is a big computer."

"No. Not a computer. A robot. Another one of us, except it is so big it has no mobility."

"We are talking to no point at all," said Red Cloud. "A robot is nothing more than a walking computer."

"There are points of difference," said Jason, gently. "That, Horace, is what you have refused to see all these years. You've thought of a robot as a machine and it is not. It is a biological concept expressed mechanically . . ."

"You are quibbling," Red Cloud said.

"I don't think we'll gain anything," said John, "even by the most good-natured argument. We didn't come here, actually, to find what might be building. We came to see how the robots would react to the People, perhaps, many of them, millions of them, coming back to Earth."

"I can tell you, without any question, how the most of us would react to it," said Stanley. "We would view it with some apprehension. For they would take us back into their service or, perhaps worse than that, would have no need of us. Some of us, perhaps quite a number of us, would welcome being taken back into their service, for through all the years we have felt the lack of someone needing us. Some of us would welcome the old servitude, for to us it was never really servitude. But I think, as well, that the majority of us now feel we have started on a road along which we can work out for ourselves something approaching the destiny of mankind—not that precise kind of destiny, of course, for it would not fit us and we would not want it. For that reason we would not want the humans to come back. They would interfere. They could not help the interference; it is intellectually impossible for them not to interfere in any affairs that touch them, even most remotely. But that is not a decision we can make for ourselves alone. The decision is the province of the Project . . ."

"You mean the monster you have built," said Hezekiah.

Stanley, who had been standing all the time, slowly lowered himself into a chair. He swiveled his head around to stare at Hezekiah. "You do not approve?" he asked. "You do not understand? Of all these people, I would have thought you would."

"You have committed sacrilege," said Hezekiah, sternly. "You have erected an abomination. You have chosen to elevate yourself above your creators. I have spent many lonely, terrible hours, wondering if I and my associates may not be committing sacrilege, devoting our time and utmost effort to a study and a task that should be mankind's study and its task, but at least we still are working for the good of mankind . . ."

"Please," said Jason. "Let us not debate that now. How can any of us tell if we're right or wrong in any of our actions? Stanley says that it is up to the Project to decide . . ."

"The Project will know," said Stanley. "It has far more background knowledge than any one of us. We have traveled widely through the years to obtain material that has been fed into its memory cores. We have given it all the knowledge it has been our fortune to lay our hands upon. It knows history, science, philosophy, the arts. And now it is adding to this knowledge on its own. It is talking with something very far in space."

John jerked upright. "How far in space?" he asked.

"We are not sure," said Stanley. "Something, we believe, in the center of the galaxy."

21

He felt the crying need of the creature in the glen, the lack of something that it sought and the damnation of that lack. He stopped so quickly that Evening Star, walking close behind, bumped into him.

"What is it?" she whispered.

He stood rigid, feeling the lack and need, and he did not answer. The wash of feeling from the glen came pouring over him and into him—the hopelessness, the doubt, the longing and the need. The trees stood straight and silent in the breathless afternoon and for a moment everything in the forest—the birds, the little animals, the insects—fell into a silence. Nothing stirring, nothing making any noise, as if all of nature held its breath to listen to the creature in the glen.

"What's wrong?" asked Evening Star.

"There is something suffering," he said. "Can't you feel the suffering? It's just there ahead of us."

"You can't feel suffering," she said.

He moved ahead slowly and the silence held and there the creature was—a terrible can of worms crouched against the nest of boulders that lay beneath the arching birch. But he did not see the can of worms, he only heard the cry of need and something turned over in his mind and for a moment he held the need within his mental grip.

Evening Star recoiled and came up against the tough bark of an oak that stood beside the path. The can of worms kept changing, exactly as a can of worms would change, all the worms crawling over one another in the seething ferment of some nameless, senseless urge. And out of that seething mass came a cry of gladness and relief—a cry of gladness and relief that had no sound at all, and a cry that somehow was intertwined with a sense of compassion and of power that had nothing to do with the can of worms. And over all of this was spread, like a mantle of hope and understanding, what the great white oak had said, or tried to say, or failed to say, and within her mind the universe opened up like a flower awakened by the rising sun. For an instant she sensed and knew (not saw or heard or understood, for it all was beyond simple sight or understanding) the universe to its very core and out to its farthest edges—the mechanism of it and the purpose of its existence and the place that was held in it by everything that held the touch of life.

Only for an instant, a fractional second of realizing, of knowing, and then unknowing, then she was back again within herself, an incomplete, insignificant life form that crouched against the tree, feeling the rough bark of the massive oak against her shoulders and her back, with David Hunt standing in the path beside her and in the glen a squirming can of worms that seemed to shine with a holy light, so bright and glittering that it was beautiful as no can of worms could ever be, and crying over and over inside her brain, with a meaning in the cry she could not comprehend.

"David," she cried, "what have we done? What happened?"

For there had been a great happening, she knew, or perhaps great happenings and she was confused, although in the confusion there was something that was at once a happiness and wonder. She crouched against the tree and the universe seemed to lean down above her and she felt hands fastening upon her and lifting her and she was in David's arms, clinging to him as she had never clung to anyone before, glad that he was there in what she sensed must be the great moment of her life, secure within the strength of his lean, hard body.

"You and I," he was saying. "You and I together. Between the two of us . . ."

His voice faltered and she knew that he was frightened and she put her arms about him and held him with all the comfort that she had.

22

They waited on the riverbank, with the canoes drawn up on the rocky beach. Some of the canoemen were squatted about a tiny driftwood fire, broiling fish that they had caught, others were sitting about and talking, one of them lay fast asleep upon the river pebbles—which seemed to Jason, watching the sleeper, to be a most unsatisfactory bed.

The river was smaller here, much smaller than it was at the old camp from which they had started out. It was in a hurry here, its waters, sparkling in the sun of late afternoon, running between high bluffs that rose on either side, the stream sliding down an imperceptible chute.

Behind them rose the great flared structure of the Project, a black thin scroll of metal that seemed at once massive from its very size and yet so fragile that one wondered it did not flutter in the breeze.

"Did the same thought cross your mind," John asked Jason, "as occurred to me?"

"You mean whatever it might be the Project was talking with?"

"That's it," said John. "Do you think that it is possible? Could a superrobot, or a vastly sophisticated computer, or whatever that thing is up there, get in contact with the Principle?"

"It may only be listening to it, be aware of it, perhaps extracting some information from it. It may not actually be talking with it."

"It does not have to be the Principle," said John. "It could be another race or other races. We have found a few of them and of these there are very few with whom we can communicate because we have no common ground for understanding. But a biological-mechanical contraption, such as that up there, might make ground for understanding. It may have a mind, if what it has can be called a mind, that is more flexible than ours. There is no question that it is the equal of mankind in its background for understanding. For hundreds of years the robots have pumped into its memory cores as much of human knowledge as they have been able to lay their hands upon. It probably is the best educated entity that has ever existed on the Earth. It has the equivalent of several hundred university or college educations. The sheer impact of the knowledge—all of which it would keep intact, not being subject to the forgetfulness of human beings—might have given it a broader outlook than any man has yet achieved."

"Whatever it is talking with," said Jason, "it is one up on us. There are very few intelligences out there with which we have been able to set up any kind of communication, let alone a meaningful communication. And the communication this superrobot has set up, I gather, is very meaningful."

"Perhaps meaningful for two reasons," said John. "First, it might be able to decipher the symbols of the language . . ."

"The function of a good computer," Jason pointed out.

"And, secondly, a good computer might have, not only a better and a different understanding, but a wider understanding. It might have a wider spectrum of understanding than is possible in a human. Our failure to achieve communication is due, in many instances, to our inability to comprehend a way of thought and a schedule of values different from our own."

"It is taking a long time," said Red Cloud. "Do you think that monstrosity up there is having trouble making up its mind? Although I'm inclined to think it makes no difference what it says. I am doubtful it could be of help."

"It is not a monstrosity, sir," said Hezekiah. "It is a logical construction for such as I to make, although I must hasten to say that such as I would never make it. Logical though it may be, it is an abomination built of sinful pride. But even so, I am certain that if it so decides, it can be of help. For, logically built, it would deal in logic . . ."

"We'll soon know," said Jason, "for Stanley is coming down the path."

They got to their feet and waited for the glittering robot. He came down off the path and across the beach to stand in front of them. He looked from one to another of them. "For you," he finally said, "the news is bad."

"You won't help us, then," said Jason.

"I am truly sorry," the robot said. "My personal inclination would be to cooperate with you in any way we could. But we built the Project as another one of us, as a greater one of us—perhaps I should say," nodding to Horace Red Cloud, "as the chief of us and in consequence must go along with the Project's judgment. For what is the sense of creating a chief if you do not trust and follow him?"

"But on what basis was the judgment made?" Jason asked. "That you do not trust us, perhaps. Or that the problem, in your opinion, is somewhat less a problem than we had stated it?"

Stanley shook his head. "Neither of those," he said.

"You realize, of course, that if the People come they can take you over. And the Project, too."

Hezekiah said, "Surely you owe these gentlemen the courtesy . . ."

"You keep out of this," said Stanley, speaking sharply.

"I will not keep out of it," said Hezekiah, his words rasping with an uncharacteristic anger. "These are the creatures that made us. They are our creators. Any loyalty that we have we owe to them. Even your Project owes them loyalty, for you used not only the intelligence that the humans gave you to conceive and build the Project, but you salvaged from their world the materials to build it, the knowledge to feed into it."

"We no longer look for loyalty," said Jason. "Perhaps we never should have. I sometimes think we owe you an apology for ever having built you. We certainly gave you no world for which you have occasion to be thankful. But now, as it turns out, we're all in this together. If the People come back to occupy the planet, all of us will suffer."

"What do you want?" asked Stanley.

"Your help, of course. But since you can't give us that, I think we have the right to ask why you are refusing help."

"It will be no comfort to you."

"Who said anything of comfort? It's not comfort we are looking for."

"All right," said Stanley. "Since you insist. But I cannot tell you."

He reached into the pouch suspended from his waist, took out a folded piece of paper, unfolded it and smoothed it out.

"This," he said, "is the answer that the Project gave us."

He handed the piece of paper to Jason. There were three printed lines upon it. They read: *The situation outlined is immaterial to us. We could help humanity, but there is no reason that we should. Humanity is a transient factor and is none of our concern.*

23

Uncle Jason had said that, as a beginning, she should read history—starting with the general histories. This, he said, would provide a basis for an understanding of all the rest of it.

Now, sitting at the desk in the library, with the night wind muttering in the eaves and the thick candle burned almost to its socket, Evening Star wondered wearily at the need of understanding. Understanding would not take the lines of worry from Uncle Jason's face. It would not ensure, if the People came, that the forests and the buffalo plains would remain, unchanged, the province of her people. And it would not tell her what had happened to David Hunt.

The last consideration, she admitted to herself, was for her, personally, the most important one of all. He had held and kissed her on that day they'd found the creature in the glen and they'd walked back to the house together hand in hand. And that had been the last she had seen of him, the last that anyone had seen of him. She had walked the woods, hoping she would find him or some trace of where he might have gone, and she remembered with a rush of shame that she had gone down the road to the monastery to inquire if he'd been there. The robots had not cared; they had been courteous, but scarcely pleasant, and she had walked back to the house feeling, in a sense, degraded, as if she had shown her naked body to those uncaring men of metal.

Had he run from her, she wondered. Or had she read more into what had happened that day in the glen than had actually been there? Both of them, she realized, had been shaken by the events that had transpired in the glen and their flooding emotions may have found an outlet in one another that was, viewed in a sober moment, entirely without meaning. She didn't think, she told herself, that had been the case. She had thought about it since and the answer seemed to be that the events had no more than triggered something that she had known and felt, but had not entirely realized—that she loved this wanderer from the west. But had he, she wondered, asked the same question of himself and found another answer?

Had he run away? Or was there something that he still must seek—after all the months and miles of seeking, was he seeking still? Was he convinced that what he hunted—perhaps not really knowing what he hunted—did not lie in this house or in herself, and had he moved on toward the east in his endless quest?

She pushed the book away from her and sat in the quietness of the shadowed library, with all its tiers of books, with the candle guttering as it burned toward its end. Winter soon would come, she thought, and he would be cold. There were blankets she could have given him, there were robes that would have kept him warm. But he had not told her he was going and there was no way she could know.

Once again she lived over in her mind that day when they had found the creature. It all had been most confusing and she found that it still was impossible to put it all together, saying that, first, this

happened, then another event took place, and after
that, another. It was all jumbled up together, as if
everything had happened all at once with no chinks
of time between them, but she knew it had not been
that way, that there had been a progression of events,
although they had happened rather fast and had not
been orderly. The oddest thing of all was that she
had trouble separating what David had done and what
she had done and she wondered, once again, if, while
they may not have done it all together, whether one
of them alone could have made any of it happen, but
that, rather, it took the two of them to do what each
had done.

And what had she done, she wondered. What had
happened to her? Trying to recall it, she could dis-
cover only fragments of it and she was sure that
when it had happened there had been no fragmenta-
tion and that the fragments she could recall were no
more than broken pieces of the whole. The world
had opened out and so had the universe, or what she
since had thought must have been the universe, lying
all spread out before her, with every nook revealed,
with all the knowledge, all the reasons there—a universe in which time and space had been ruled out
because time and space were only put there, in the
first place, to make it impossible for anyone to grasp
the universe. Seen for a moment, half-sensed, a flash
of insight that had been gone before there had been
time for it to register on her brain, sensed and known
for an instant only and then gone so quickly that it
had left impression only, no certain memory and no
solid knowledge, but impressions only, like a face
seen in a lightning flash and then the darkness closing
in.

Was this—could this—be the realization of what
she had tried to tell Grandfather Oak, knowing that
there was something happening inside her, that
change was about to come, but not knowing what it
was and telling him instead that she might go away

again, although in a different sense than she had
gone to the wild rice country? If that were the case,
she thought, if this were it, if this might be a new
ability, like going to the stars, and not simply something that she had imagined, she'd never have to
go anywhere again, for she was already there, she
was any place that she might want to be.

It was the first time she had thought of it as an
ability and she found herself confused and frightened,
not so much at the implications of the thought as that
she had thought of it at all, that she, even subcon-
sciously, could have allowed herself to think of it.
She sat stiff and straight, holding herself tense, and
in the shadowed room flickering with the light of the
dying candle, she seemed to hear again the muttering
and stirring of all those ghosts that huddled there
among their works, the one last place left to them on
Earth.

24

(Excerpt from journal of Nov. 29, 5036) . . . In the last few centuries I have experienced some physical deterioration and now there are days (like today) when I feel the weight of years upon me. I have a tiredness that cannot be accounted for by usual exertion, for I never have exerted myself too greatly and late years almost not at all. My step has been reduced to shuffling and my hand, once firm, has lost some coordination, so that the writing in this journal has become shaky scrawling and there are times, as well, when I write a word I do not mean to write—a word very close to the one I meant to write, but not the one intended. There are other times when I cannot think of the word I want and must sit here sifting back through memory for it, saddened rather than irritated that I cannot think of it. I misspell a word at times, which is something I never used to do. I have become, I think, like an old dog sleeping in the sun, with the significant difference that the old dog expects nothing of itself.

Alison, my wife, passed away five hundred years ago and while I cannot recall a great deal now, I remember that her death was a peaceful dying and I would presume that mine may be the same. Living as a human being now lives, death comes by wearing out and not by the ravages of disease and this, more than the long life, I think, is the real blessing that has been conferred upon us. There are times when I wonder just how much a boon the longer life—the fabulously longer life—has been to humankind. Although such thoughts, I tell myself, are the crotchety views of an aging being, and in consequence to be given little credence.

One thing I do recall, and ever since that day it has haunted me. When Alison died many people came, from far among the stars, and we had a service for her, in the house, and at the graveside. There being no person of religious calling, my grandson Jason read from the Bible and said the words that custom decreed should be said and it all was very solemn and, in many ways, most satisfactory. The humans stood at the graveside, a great crowd of us, and at a little distance the robots stood, not that we had indicated in any way that they should stand apart, but of their own choosing and according to the ancient custom.

After it all was over, we went back to the house and after a time I retired into the library and sat there alone, no one intruding on me, for they understood my need to be alone. After a time there was a knock upon the door and when I called out for whoever it was to enter, in came Hezekiah of the monastery. He had come to tell me that he and his companions had not been at the funeral (a fact that I had failed to notice) because at the time those of the monastery had held a memorial service for her. Having told me this, he presented me with a copy of the service they had held. It was lettered on the sheets most legibly and beautifully, with colorful illustrative initials and decorations around the margins of the pages—the same careful, meticulous kind of manuscript as had been turned out in the scriptoriums of the Middle Ages. Frankly, I did not know how to respond. It was impudent of him, of course, and from my viewpoint not in the best of taste. But there was no question that what he and his companions had done had been with no thought of impudence nor impropriety, but from their own light, an act of utmost charity. So I thanked him and I fear I was somewhat curt in the thanks and I am certain he noted the curtness. At the time I did not record the incident in the journal and never spoke of it to anyone. I doubt that anyone, in fact, was aware that the robot had come calling on me. Over the years I have been most responsible in the writing of everything that happens. At first I started the journal so that the truth of what had happened to the human race would be placed upon the record and thus serve as a deterrent against the rise of myth and legend. I think that at the time I had no other reason and did not plan to continue with the journal, but by the time I had it all written down I had so acquired the habit of writing that I continued with it, putting down upon the pages all daily events, however small, as they took place—oftentimes writing down my thoughts as well as the events. Why I did not record at the time what took place between myself and Hezekiah has been a long, long puzzle to me. Surely it did not carry so great a significance, did not constitute so great a breach of etiquette, that it must be hidden. At first I put it out of my mind and when I happened to think of it, put it out of my mind again, but of late it has been with me overmuch.

In the last few years I have been able to ask myself many questions concerning the incident, for now the edge of the encounter has dulled and I can think of it objectively. The thought has occurred to me that we might have considered asking Hezekiah to officiate at the funeral, he rather than Jason reading the burial service and the words of comfort, although, shying from this even now, I know it would have been impossible then. And yet the fact remains that

A Choice of Gods 153

robot, rather than man, has kept not only Christianity, but the very idea of religion alive. This may not be entirely true, I realize, for Red Cloud's people undoubtedly do have a body of beliefs and a pattern of attitude that should be called religion, although as I understand it, it is not formalized, but is highly personal—which probably makes for a better practice and more common sense than the empty formalizations that other religions had become. But the point, it seems to me, is that we should either have held to our religion or have abandoned it entirely. What we did was let it die because we no longer cared and had grown very weary of pretending to believe. This does not apply to the last few thousand years alone. Even before the Disappearance our faith had been allowed to die and in this sense I use the word faith in a most restrictive sense, equating it with organized religion.

I have thought much on this the last number of years, sitting on the patio and watching the seasons pass. In the process I have become a student of the sky and know all the clouds there are and have firmly fixed in mind the various hues of blue that the sky can show—the washed-out, almost invisible blue of a hot, summer noon; the soft robin's egg, sometimes almost greenish blue of a late springtime evening, the darker, almost violet blue of fall. I have become a connoisseur of the coloring that the leaves take on in autumn and I know all the voices and the moods of the woods and river valley. I have, in a measure, entered into communion with nature, and in this wise have followed in the footsteps of Red Cloud and his people, although I am sure that their understanding and their emotions are more fine-tuned than mine are. I have seen, however, the roll of seasons, the birth and death of leaves, the glitter of the stars on more nights than I can number and from all this as from nothing else I have gained a sense of a purpose and an orderliness which it does not seem to me can have stemmed from accident alone.

It seems to me, thinking of it, that there must be some universal plan which set in motion the orbiting of the electrons about the nucleus and the slower, more majestic orbit of the galaxies about one another to the very edge of space. There is a plan, it seems to me, that reaches out from the electron to the rim of the universe and what this plan may be or how it came about is beyond my feeble intellect. But if we are looking for something on which to pin our faith—and, indeed, our hope—the plan might well be it. I think we have thought too small and have been too afraid . . .

25

The concert came to a crashing close and the music trees stood silent in the autumn moonlight. Down in the river valley owls were chuckling back and forth to one another and a faint breeze sent a rustle through the leaves. Jason stirred in his chair, glancing over his shoulder at the great antenna that had been installed upon the roof, then settled back again.

Martha rose from her chair. "I am going in," she said. "Are you coming, Jason?"

"I think I'll stay here for a while," he said. "We don't get too many nights like this, this late in the year. It's a shame to miss it. Do you happen to know where John is? He didn't come out tonight."

"John is getting restless with the waiting," Martha said. "One of these days he will be off to the stars again. He has found, I imagine, this is home no longer. He has been gone too long."

Jason grumbled at her. "No place is home to John. He hasn't got a home. He doesn't want a home. He simply wants to wander. He's like all the rest of them. None of them, no single one of them, cares what happens to the Earth."

"They all are most sympathetic. All of those I talked with. If they could do anything, they said . . ."

"Knowing," Jason said, "there is nothing they can do."

"I suppose so. Don't take it so hard, Jason. You may be worrying about something that will never come about."

"It's not us I'm worried over," he told her. "It is Red Cloud's people and the robots. Yes, even the robots. They've made a new start of sorts. They should have their chance. There should be no interference."

"But they refused to help."

"They installed the radio and the beam," he said.

"But no real help."

"No real help," he agreed. "I can't understand the robots. I never have been able to."

"Our own robots . . ."

"Our own robots are different," Jason said. "They are a part of us. They're doing what they were intended for. They have not changed, but the others have. Hezekiah, for example . . ."

"They had to change," said Martha. "They had no choice. They couldn't hunker down and wait."

"I suppose you're right," said Jason.

"I am going in now. Don't stay out too long. It will be getting cold soon . . ."

"Where is Evening Star? She didn't come out, either. Just the two of us tonight."

"Evening Star is worrying. About that funny boy. I don't know what she sees in him."

"She has no idea what happened to him? Where he may have gone?"

"If she had, she'd not be worrying. I imagine that she thinks he ran away from her."

"You talked with her?"

"Not about the boy."

"He was a strange one," Jason said.

"Well, I'm going in. You'll be coming soon?"

He sat and listened to her footsteps going across the patio, heard the door shut behind her.

Strange about the boy, he thought, strange that he should disappear. The alien in the glen had disappeared as well. He'd gone down to see it and talk with it again and there had been no sign of it, no matter how he'd hunted. Had it grown tired of waiting and gone away, he wondered. Or could there be some connection between its disappearance and that of David Hunt? It seemed impossible that there should be; David Hunt had not known about the creature in the glen. There was this story that the lad had told of the Dark Walker and it had been quite apparent he was afraid of it and, although he did not say so, he might have crossed the continent to get away from it, to shake it from his footsteps. He might be fleeing it still—from a thing that more than likely did not exist. But that was not strange, Jason told himself. He'd not be the first to flee from a nonexistent thing.

Could it be, he wondered, that his own fear was based upon a nonexistent premise? Might it be that a reconnaissance ship carrying representatives of the People posed no actual threat to Earth? And even should it carry the seeds of change for Earth, who was he to decide that it was a threat? But that must be wrong, he thought; it could be nothing but a threat. No threat, of course, to those people who had gone out to the stars, for they had cut their ties with Earth, they no longer cared for Earth and whatever might happen on the Earth would have no impact upon them. Learning this had been something of a shock, he admitted to himself. For all the years he had fostered the idea that he had been the anchor man of Earth, that he had held in trust the home base of humanity. Now it seemed that this had been a self-sustained illusion he had nourished carefully to bolster a sense of his own importance. So far as the people of this house might be concerned, there were only he and Martha who could be harmed if the People should decide to recolonize the Earth.

And no matter how he might rebel against the thought of it, to the two of them it would not matter too much. So far as he and Martha were concerned, the People could be held at arm's length—certainly they could not interfere with this house and these few acres if it were amply apparent that they were not welcome. The very thought of them being here upon the planet would be gall upon his tongue, but it was selfishness, an utter arrogance and selfishness.

What did matter, he told himself, were the Indians, the descendants of the old aborigines who at one time had called this continent their home—and the robots as well as the Indians. Neither of them had asked for the kind of culture and civilization that had been forced upon them; the robots had not even asked for life. Enough injustice had been visited upon each of them in the past; it was more than decency could bear that they be made the victims of a new injustice. They had to have their chance. And if the People came they would have no chance.

What was this fatal disease that his own race carried? Fatal not to itself, but to all others that came in contact with it, although in the end, perhaps, fatal even to itself. It had all begun, he told himself, when the first man had scratched the ground and planted seed and must, therefore, secure to himself the ground in which to plant the seed. It had started with the concept of ownership—ownership of land, ownership of natural resources, ownership of labor. And perhaps from the concept of security as well, the erecting of fences against the adversities of life, the protection of one's station in life and the ambition to improve that station and, obtaining that improvement, to fortify it so well against one's neighbors that they could never wrest it from one. Thinking of it, he felt certain that the idea of security must, in its first instance, have risen from the concept of ownership. The two sprang from the same roots, really were the same. The man who owned was safe.

The Indians owned not one foot of ground, would spurn such ownership, for ownership would have meant they were tied to what they owned. And the robots, he wondered—did they in some manner which he had not noticed, have some idea of ownership? He doubted it very much. Their society must be even more a communistic one than the society of Red Cloud's people. It was only his own people who held to ownership, and that was the sickness in them. But it was from this sickness, built upon the basis of this sickness, that a most complicated social structure had been built up through the ages.

The social structure, swept away by the Disappearance, might be reestablished now on Earth, and what could be done about it? What could he, Jason Whitney, do to prevent it being reestablished? There was no answer, none that he could find.

The robots were a puzzle. Stanley had said that he and his fellows were deeply concerned and yet when the Project had decided against offering help they had accepted the decision without question. Although they had been helpful in a most important way. They had supplied and installed the directional beam and the radio and batteries that operated them. Without such a setup it would have been impossible to contact the People when they arrived. Without the directional beam it would have been highly probable that they could arrive and leave without ever knowing there were people on the planet. They would land, perhaps at several places, make their surveys and then return to their new home planets to report that Earth was uninhabited. And it was important, Jason told himself—terribly important—that he have a chance to talk with them. What he could do by talking he had no idea, but at least he must have this chance to talk with those men on the ship that must, by now, be coming near to Earth. With the homing beam reaching out in space they would know there still were people here and would have means to seek them out.

Jason sat huddled in his chair. He felt lonely and forsaken; once again he wondered if he could be mistaken in all of this, and brushed the thought away. Mistaken for himself, perhaps, even mistaken for the robots, but certainly not mistaken for Red Cloud and his people—and perhaps not for himself or the robots, either.

He tried deliberately to wipe his mind clear of the whole affair. Perhaps if he could wipe it clean and keep it clean for a little while, he could think the clearer when the time came to think again. He sat as easily as he could, not thinking, willing the tenseness in him to soften and relax. He saw the moon glinting off the roofs of the monastery buildings and making slim white ghosts of the music trees. The last few nights, he thought, the trees had done much better, as good or even better than in the days of long ago. Their improvement had come about, he recalled, in the middle of the concert on the evening of the day his brother John had come home from the stars. He had noticed it then and had wondered over it for a little time, but there had been too much to do, too much to worry over, to think of it for long. On the night of the day John came home, he thought, but the fact of the homecoming could not have a thing to do with it. John's coming home could have made no difference to the music trees.

A foot crunched on the paving stones and Jason swung around in his chair. Thatcher was hurrying toward him.

"Mr. Jason, sir," the robot said, "there is someone calling on the radio. I told him to wait and I would put you on."

Jason rose from the chair. He was aware of a weakness in his knees, a goneness in his belly. This was it, he thought, this was it at last. He wasn't ready for it. He would never, he realized, have been ready for it.

"Thank you, Thatcher," he said. "There is something I'd like you to do for me."

"Anything at all, sir." Thatcher was excited. Jason looked at him curiously—he had never thought he'd see Thatcher excited.

"Would you please send one of the robots down to Red Cloud's camp. Tell him what has happened. Tell him that I need him. Ask him if he'll come."

"Immediately," said Thatcher. "I'll make the trip myself."

"That is fine," said Jason. "I had hoped you would. Horace knows you. He might resent any other robot yelling him awake."

Thatcher turned and started off.

"Just a moment," Jason said. "There is something further. Would you ask Red Cloud to send someone up the river and fetch Stanley down. We should have him here. And Hezekiah, too. One of the other robots can rout out Hezekiah."

26

He had killed that last bear when it had been so close that there had been no time to get off a decent shot. He had killed all the others, too—one bear for each of the claws in the necklace that hung about his throat. Some of the others, perhaps all of them, had been killed by the arrows he had fired—stout, true, well-fletched arrows driven by a powerful bow. But now he could not be sure, not absolutely sure, about the arrows.

Although it was not only killing. It was healing, too.

He had killed the bears, but he had healed the trees. He had thought so at the time and now he was sure he had. He had sensed something wrong with them and he had made it right, although he had never really known what had been wrong with them.

The alien came hobbling through the moonlit trees and squatted close to him. It made the worms go round and round and tumble all about. It had been following him for days and he was weary of it.

"Get out of here," he yelled. "Go away," he shouted.

It paid no attention. It stayed there, redistributing the worms. He had been tempted at times to do to it whatever it was he had done to the bears. But he told himself that it would not be right to do it to the alien. The alien was no real threat, or at least he didn't think it was; it was just a nuisance.

The alien squirmed closer.

"I gave you what you wanted," shouted David Hunt at it. "I fixed up what was wrong with you. I took away the ache. Now leave me alone."

The alien backed away.

David crouched at the foot of the mighty maple and tried to think it out—although, actually, there was not too much to think about. The record seemed quite clear: He had cured the trees, he had cured this strange creature which continually came sneaking up on him, he had cured the bird of its broken wing and an old black bear of an aching tooth and he had purged a bed of asters of a deadly thing that sucked the life from them (and was not quite easy in his mind on that one, for in helping the asters it appeared that he had killed some other form of life —a lowly life perhaps, but it still was life). As if a great compassion came rolling out of him to make all things well and whole and yet, quite strangely, he felt no great compassion. Rather, he felt an uneasiness when he sensed an unwell or aching thing and somehow he must make it right again. Right, perhaps, so he'd not be bothered with it. Was he to go through life, he wondered, sensing all the wrongness with the world? He had been all right until that night he had listened to the trees—until he had sensed the wrongness in them, he had been oblivious to wrongness, had not been aware of wrongness and quite carefree because he did not know of it. Something in the music, he wondered. Something in the robot that had stood beside him? And what did it mean, he wondered—that he must go stumbling through life aware of every little trouble, every little ill, and could get no rest or peace until he had fixed them all?

Out of the corner of his eye, David Hunt saw the alien creeping closer. He waved his hands at it in a pantomime of pushing it away.

"Get out of here!" he yelled.

27

Jason picked up the microphone and thumbed the switch. And what did one say, he wondered. Was there a convention of radio conversation? If so, he didn't know it.

He said, "This is Jason Whitney of the planet Earth. Are you still out there?"

He waited and after a pause the voice came: "Jason who? Please identify."

"Jason Whitney."

"Whitney. Are you a human? Or another robot?"

"I am human," Jason said.

"Are you qualified to talk with us?"

"I am the only one who can. I'm the only human here."

"The only . . ."

"There are other humans. Not many. Only a few of us. At the moment the others are not here."

The voice was puzzled, but it said, "Yes, we understand. We were told there were few humans. A few humans only and some robots."

Jason sucked in his breath, cutting off the questions that came unbidden to his tongue. How would you know? Who told you there were humans? Certainly not John. And if any of the others out in space had found the People, they would come posting back to Earth to bring the news as quickly as they could, just as John had done. No one would have found the People and talked with them casually and then gone on without getting word to Earth.

Should he let them know, he wondered, that their coming had been anticipated? Like how come it took so long, we had expected you much sooner. That would set them back on their heels exactly as they had set him back on his. But he throttled the desire. He could tell them nothing now. It might be to Earth's advantage if they did not know.

"We had not expected," said the voice, "to find a directional beam or a radio. Once we found the beam, of course . . ."

"Our robots," Jason said, "use radios to talk back and forth."

"But the beam . . ."

"I see no reason why you and I should argue," Jason told them smoothly. "Especially since I have no idea who you are."

"But the beam . . ."

"Just on the bare chance," said Jason, "that someone might want to visit us. It takes little effort to keep it operational. Now please identify yourself. Tell me who you are."

"We once lived on Earth," the voice said. "We were taken from it long ago. Now we are coming back."

"Then," said Jason, calmly, "you must be the People. We had wondered, all these years, what could have happened to you."

"The People?"

"That is what we called you—if you are the ones who disappeared from Earth."

"We are the ones."

"Well, welcome back," said Jason.

He smiled quietly to himself. As if they'd just stepped across the road to visit friends and were late in getting back. It could not be the way they had expected it. What they had expected, more than likely, was a sort of gibbering joy that they had found their way back to Earth and that after all the years the poor creatures who had been left behind were united once again with others of their race.

"We had expected we would have to hunt for you," the voice said. "We had feared, in fact, that we would not find you."

Jason chuckled. "You have been spared that fear. Are you coming in to visit us? I don't quite see how you can. We have no landing field."

"We need no field. We'll send down a boat, with two men. The boat can land anywhere. Just keep the beam going. The boat will ride it down."

"There's a cornfield near the house," said Jason. "You'll recognize it by the corn shocks. You can manage there?"

"Very nicely."

"When can we be expecting you?"

"By morning light."

"In that case," said Jason, "we'll kill the fatted calf."

Alarm sounded in the voice. "You'll do what?" it asked.

"Never mind," said Jason. "Just a saying. We'll be seeing you."

28

The oak log finally burned through and broke into two pieces, collapsing, sending up a shower of sparks that funneled up the chimney. The wind growled in the flue and from far off came the whining of the eaves. They sat by the fire and waited, the three of them—Martha, John and Jason.

"It worries me," said Jason. "How did they come to know? How could they have learned there was anybody here? It must have been quite natural for them to have assumed the entire race was taken. By rights, they should have thought they were coming to a planet with no inhabitants. They would have known, at least assumed, that the robots had been left behind and that they would have guessed the robots would persist. They might logically have imagined they'd find a robot civilization, but they couldn't know . . ."

"Don't worry about it," said John. "We'll get the answer soon enough. The important thing is that you handled it just right. You left them guessing. They must be mighty puzzled people. Your reactions were not typical to the situation and you've got them worried. They don't know what to think. They're up there psyching you right now."

"No matter what," said Martha, "you shouldn't take on so. This is no life and death affair."

"To me it is," said Jason. "And it is to Red Cloud. We can't let them ruin everything."

"Maybe they won't," said Martha.

"Another planet for them to take over," Jason said. "Do you think they'd miss a chance like that?"

"But a planet," suggested John, "with its resources stripped. They know the planet has been stripped; they stripped it."

"Minerals, of course," said Jason. "The minerals are gone and most of the fossil fuels. Although they probably could salvage a lot of the minerals from the ruins—it's not all gone back to rust. And the cities would be quarries for building stone. Since the Disappearance the forests have grown up again. The forests today can't be much inferior to what they were when the Europeans took over the continent. The same would be true of the rest of the world. Back to primordial woodlands. Billions of board feet of lumber. The land has renewed itself. It's fertile once again, as it was before man first scratched the earth to plant a crop. The sea is full of fish."

"We can bargain with them," Martha said. "We can talk with them."

"We have nothing to bargain with," said Jason, bitterly. "We can appeal to their better nature, but I have no hope in that."

Footsteps came clumping down the hall. Jason leaped to his feet.

"It's only Hezekiah," Martha said. "Thatcher sent him word."

Hezekiah came into the room. "There was no one," he said, "to announce my coming. I hope I do no wrong."

"Of course you haven't," Martha said. "Thank you for coming. Won't you please sit down."

"I do not need to sit," said Hezekiah, primly.

"Damn it, Hezekiah," Jason said, "stop practicing your humility on us. In this house you're like any of the rest of us."

"I thank you, Mr. Jason," Hezekiah said. He sat down on a sofa. "I must admit that I have become partial to this human thing of sitting. In my case there is no earthly reason for it, but I enjoy it, although I suspect my enjoyment of it is something of a sin. I am told you have received word from the coming People. Aside from my realization of the problem posed by their imminent arrival, I am considerably intrigued at the opportunity to get from them some account of the development of their belief in the matter of religion. It would be a comfort . . ."

"You will find no comfort," John told him. "You can hope for nothing from them. I saw no evidence of any religious belief while I was on their planet."

"No evidence at all, sir?"

"None at all," said John. "No churches, no places of worship, no inclination to worship. No ministers or preachers or priests. And don't act so startled. Certainly it would be possible for a society to exist, quite comfortably, without any kind of faith. In fact, even before the Disappearance, we almost did. And in case you are wondering, there is no evidence that the lack of faith had anything to do with the Disappearance."

"I don't care too much about what they believe or don't believe," said Jason. "Let's not get off the track. How could the People have known there was anybody here? John, you didn't, by any chance . . ."

"No," said John. "I am sure I didn't. I did my best not to give any inkling that I came from Earth. I'm almost positive I said nothing . . ."

"How, then? No other of our people have been there. If they had been, they would have told us. It wouldn't be something that anyone would ignore.

All these years we have wondered what happened to the People. It is a question that never has been too far from our thoughts."

"Have you considered that the People may have heard it from some other intelligence? We've been at no pains, as we traveled in the galaxy, to hide where we are from or how we travel . . ."

"Then you think they could know, as well, about our star-traveling?"

"It is possible," said John. "Remember, the People are star rovers, too. They have their ships. They may have visited many planets. I know they have made star trips. In the course of their traveling, they could have contacted some intelligences, probably among them some of the same we have contacted."

"Our contacts have not been too satisfactory."

"Nor, perhaps, have theirs. But if they developed any contact at all with the intelligences we have met, one of the first things they would learn would be that others like them had visited the planet and by an entirely different means than they used in getting there. These People are not stupid, Jason. They could put two and two together."

"But you heard none of this. Nothing to hint at it. All the time you spent on their planet, you heard nothing at all."

John shook his head. "Only that they finally had relocated Earth and some months since had sent out a survey ship to visit it. You must realize, however, that I was in no position to reach into their governmental or scientific circles. All I heard was what the common people knew or could read in their publications."

"You think if the government knew about it they might have kept their knowledge secret?"

"They could have. I don't know what the reason for secrecy could have been, but it's possible."

Soft feet came down the hall toward the room in which they sat.

"That's Red Cloud," said Jason. He rose and met his old friend as he came into the room.

"I'm sorry to rout you out, Horace," he said, "but they'll be here this morning."

"I would not," said Horace Red Cloud, "have missed this wake for all the world."

"Wake?"

"Certainly. The custom of old barbarians from across the sea. No Indian foolishness."

"You mean sitting with the dead."

"And this time," said Horace, "the dead are a planet and a people. My planet and my people."

"They may have changed," said Martha. "They've had thousands of years to acquire some different viewpoints, a new morality, to mature a little. It might be a different culture."

Red Cloud shook his head. "John, from what he told us, doesn't seem to think so. He spent some time with them and it's the same old culture, a little smarter, maybe, a little slicker in its operations. These kind never change. A machine does something to a man. It brutalizes him. It serves as a buffer between himself and his environment and he is the worst for it. It arouses an opportunistic instinct and makes possible a greed that makes a man inhuman."

"I'm frightened," Jason said, "if that's what you want to hear me say."

"I sent a canoe up the river," said Red Cloud, "to carry word to Stanley—I think that is his name. Although why we bother with him I do not understand."

"We're all in this together. He has a right to be here if he wants to come."

"Remember what that contraption said? We are a transient factor . . ."

"I suppose we are," said Jason. "The trilobites

were a transient factor. So were the dinosaurs. I suppose the robots have the right to think—even good reason to believe—they'll outlive us all."

"If they do," said Red Cloud, "it will serve them right."

29

They arrived at dawn, their little craft landing softly in the cornfield. In coming to a landing, it knocked down and scattered a corn shock and smashed three pumpkins. The little band of four humans and one robot waited at the edge of the field. There were other robots about, Jason knew, but well hidden, peering out in awe at this machine that came down from the sky. When the hatch opened, two men stepped out. They were tall and heavy, dressed in plain gray pants and jackets, small caps on their heads.

Jason strode down to the field toward them. They came to meet him.

"You are Jason Whitney," said one of them. "The one who talked with us last night."

"Yes, I am," said Jason. "Welcome back to Earth."

"I am Reynolds," said one of them, holding out his hand. "My companion is Harrison."

Jason shook hands with the two of them.

"We are not armed," said Harrison, "but we have protection." It was almost as if the speech was ritual.

"You have no need of protection here," said Jason. "We are highly civilized. There is not an ounce of violence in all of us combined."

"One never knows," said Harrison. "After all, we have been apart for some thousands of years, time enough for change. Not an alien encounter, of course, but with some aspects that are not too far from it. You tried last night, Mr. Whitney, to throw us in confusion."

"I do not understand," said Jason.

"Your words are calculated to make us believe you had no notice of our coming. I don't know how you could have had, but it was apparent that you knew. You studiously showed no surprise and if you had not known, you would have been surprised. You attempted to make it seem our arrival was of little consequence."

"Should it be of consequence?" asked Jason.

"We can offer much to you."

"We are satisfied," said Jason, "with the little that we have."

"There was the beam," said Harrison. "You would not have had a beam out if you had not believed there was someone out there. There is very little traffic in this part of the galaxy."

"You gentlemen," said Jason, "seem to be sure enough of your deductions to allow for rudeness."

"We do not mean to be rude," Reynolds said. "We do think there should be understanding. You attempted to mislead us and it might clear the way for further talk if we let you know that we realize the situation."

"You are our guests," said Jason. "I don't intend to bicker with you. If you believe what you say, there is no possible way in which I could persuade you otherwise, and, indeed, no point in doing so."

"We were somewhat surprised," said Harrison, casually conversational, "to learn, a little time ago, there were humans still on Earth. We had realized, of course, that there must be robots, for whatever it was that swept us away did not sweep the robots.

But we had thought, of course, that there'd be no humans. We thought they got us all."

"They?" asked Jason. "Then you know who did it."

"Not at all," said Harrison. "In saying they, I may be guilty of personalizing some force that was not personal at all. We had hoped you might have some idea. We know you've traveled far. Much farther than we have."

So they knew, thought Jason, bleakly, about star-traveling. It had been too much to hope they wouldn't.

"Not I," he said. "I have never left the Earth. I have stayed at home."

"But others have."

"Yes," said Jason. "Many others."

"And they talk? Telepathy?"

"Yes, of course," said Jason.

There was no use denying it. They had learned the entire story. Maybe not heard it, not been told it. Perhaps only bits and pieces. And they'd put it all together. A handful of tiny facts and they would have the story. A new ability, he wondered—a better psychology, a sense of hunch, prognostication?

"We should have gotten together sooner," said Harrison.

"I don't understand," said Jason.

"Why, man," said Harrison, "you have got it made. So have we. The two of us together . . ."

"Please," said Jason. "The others are waiting for us. We can't stand here, talking. After you have met them, there will be breakfast. Thatcher is cooking up some pancakes."

30

(Excerpt from journal of Aug. 23, 5152) . . .
When a man gets old (and now I am getting old) it
seems he climbs a mountain to leave everyone behind, although I would suspect, if he but stopped to
think of it, he'd realize he was the one who was left
behind. In my circumstance the situation is not really
applicable, for I and all the rest of us were left behind 3,000 years ago. But in a normal human community such as existed before the Disappearance, the
old were left behind. Their old friends died or moved
away or simply went away, moving so quietly and so
softly, like leaves dried to paper thinness blowing in
the wind, that they were not missed until sometime
after they were gone and the old man (or the old
leaf), looking for them, would find with some aston-
ishment and sadness that they were not anywhere,
nor had they been for a long time in the past. He
(the old man) might ask someone where they had
gone or what had happened to them, and getting no
answer, would not ask again. For the old do not
really mind; in a strange way they become sufficient
to themselves. They need so very little and they care
so very little. They climb the mountain no one else
can see and as they climb the old, once-valued
things they've carried all their lives tend to drop

away and as they climb the higher the knapsack that they carry becomes emptier, but perhaps no less in weight than it had ever been, and the few things that are left in it, they find, with some amusement, are those few indispensable belongings which they've gathered in a long lifetime of effort and of seeking. They wonder greatly, if they think of it at all, how it was left to age to winnow out the chaff they've carried all the years, thinking that it was valuable when it was only chaff. When they reach the mountain top, they find they can see farther than they've ever seen before and with greater clarity and, if by this time they're not past all caring, may bemoan that they must approach the end of their lives before they can see with this marvelous clarity, which does little for them now, but might, in earlier years, have been of incalculable value.

Sitting here, I think of this and know there is not as much fantasy in such a notion as someone of more youthful years might believe. It seems to me that even now I can see farther and with greater clarity, although perhaps neither so far nor so clear as may be the case closer to the end. For, as yet, I cannot discern what I am looking for—the path and promise for the mankind that I know.

At the time of the Disappearance we took a different path than the one that Man had followed through the ages. We were forced, in fact, to take another path. We no longer could continue as we had before. The old world came crashing down about us and there was little left. We thought, at first, that we were lost and indeed we were, if lostness means the losing of a culture we'd built up so laboriously through the years. And yet, in time, I think we came to know that the losing of it was not entirely bad— perhaps not bad at all, but good. For the loss had been the loss of many things we were better off without. Rather than losing, we gained a chance for a second start.

I must confess that I am still somewhat confused by what we did with this second start, or rather what the second start did to us. For certainly what we did came about through no conscious effort. It happened to us. Not to me, of course, but to the others. I was, I suspect, too old, too molded in that older, earlier life, for it to happen. I stood aside, not particularly because I wanted to, but because there was no choice.

The important aspect of the whole situation, it seems to me, is that this business of traveling to the stars and talking back and forth across the galaxy (Martha, at this moment, has spent a good part of the afternoon gossiping across light years) is no more than a bare beginning. It may be that star-traveling and telepathy are the easy part of what has happened to us. They may be only the first easy steps, as hammering out a stone fist ax was the first and easy step toward the great technology that was later hammered out.

What comes next, I ask myself, and I do not know. There seems to be no logical progression to this sort of thing and the reason that there is no logic is that we are too new at it to have an understanding of what may be involved. The flint worker of prehistoric days had no idea why a stone would cleave in the fashion that he wished when he struck a blow in a certain place upon its face. He knew how, but not why, and he didn't spend much time, I would suppose, in figuring out the why. But as the cleaving of the flint came clear to men of later days, the mechanism of the parapsychic ability some millennia from now will come as clear to the men then living.

As it stands at the moment, I can only speculate. Speculation is a footless endeavor, I am well aware, but I cannot refrain from it. Standing on my mountain top, I strain my eyes to look into the future.

Will there come a time, perhaps, when a race of godlike men can manipulate the very fabric of the universe? Will they be able to rearrange the atoms, bending their structures and their energies to the will of mind alone? Will they be able to save a star tottering close to the nova stage from its natural evolutionary course and enable it to continue as a normal, stable star? Will they be able, by the power of mind alone, to engineer a planet, converting it from a useless mass of matter to an abode for life? Will they be able to alter the genetics of a life form, by the power of mind alone, refashioning it into a more significant and more satisfactory life form? Perhaps more importantly, will they be able to free the minds of universal intelligences from the chains and shackles that they carry from the olden days of their evolutionary cycle so that the intelligences become reasonable and compassionate intelligences?

It is good to dream and there could be the hope, of course, that this all might come about, man finally emerging as a factor in introducing even a great orderliness into the universe. But I cannot see the path to reach this time. I can see the beginning and can dream the hoped-for end, but the in-between escapes me. Before such a situation can obtain there must be certain progress made. It is the shape of this progress I cannot determine. We must, of course, not only know, but understand the universe before we can manipulate it and we must arrive at the ability for that manipulation by a road for which there is no map. All must necessarily come by slow degree; we shall travel that unmapped road foot by weary foot. We must grow into this new ability of ours to make things happen without the aid of silly mechanical contrivances and the growth will not be rapid.

In my far view from the mountain of my age, I seem to see an end to it, a point beyond which we cannot or, perhaps, would not wish to go. Beyond which we might not dare to go. But I do not think there will be an end to it any more than there was an end to technology, until that day something took a hand and put an end to it here on the planet of its origin. Let alone, man himself would not have ended it. Man must always take that extra or that final step, finding once he has taken it it is not a final step. Today I can imagine only so far into the future, not having the data to extend my imagery beyond a certain point. But by the time man reaches that point where my imagination fails, he will have the data to push the point far into the future. There will be no place to stop.

If man persists, there'll be no stopping him. The question, it seems to me, is not whether he will persist, but whether he has the right to. I shudder when I envision man, the prehistoric monster, continuing into a time and world where he has no place . . .

31

"I do not know," Harrison said to Jason, "how I can talk reason to you. All we want is to send a small group of people here so they can learn the parapsychic abilities, in return for which . . ."

"I have already told you," Jason said, "that we cannot teach you the abilities. It's apparent you refuse to believe what I have told you."

"I think," said Harrison, "that you are bluffing. So, all right, you're bluffing. What more do you want? Tell me what you want."

"You have nothing that we want," said Jason. "That's something else you won't believe. Let me spell it out to you once again. You either are parapsychic or you aren't. You are technological or you aren't. You can't be both of them. They are mutually exclusive because so long as you remain technological, you can't be parapsychic and once you're parapsychic you have no use for technology. We do not want any of you here under the pretense of learning what we know or can do, even if you think you want what we know or can do. A few of you, you say, and it would be a few at first, then more of you, and after that still more and once you understand there was no chance of going parapsychic, why, then, you'd settle in. It's the pattern of technology—to grab and hold, then grab and hold some more . . ."

"But if we were sincere," protested Reynolds. "If we really meant it. And, of course, we do. We are being honest with you." .

"I have told you it can't be done," said Jason. "If you want to be parapsychic, you don't have to come to Earth. Let those people who want to be parapsychic strip themselves of everything they have, let them live thus stripped for two thousand years. At the end of that time it might happen to them, although I'll not guarantee it. We didn't know of it until it happened to us. It was easier for us than it would be for you. There'd be a difference in the attitude of people who set out deliberately to acquire the abilities and that difference in attitude might make it impossible."

"What you are talking about," said John, "is a combination of your way of life with ours. You see a great advantage to both of us if it could be done. If some of your people could only find the way, you'd figure that you had it made. But it wouldn't work. If some of your people could become parapsychic, they'd stand alien from you; they'd take the same attitude toward you that we are taking now."

Harrison looked around the table slowly and deliberately, at each one sitting there. "Your arrogance is appalling," he said.

"We are not arrogant," said Martha. "We are so far from arrogant . . ."

"But you are," said Harrison. "You assume that you are better now than you were before. How better I don't know, but better. You hold technology in contempt. You view it with disdain, and perhaps alarm, forgetting that if it had not been for technology we'd all be squatting in a cave."

"Perhaps not," said Jason. "If we'd not cluttered up our lives with machines . . ."

"But you don't know that."

"No, of course I don't," said Jason.

"So we should forget our squabbling," said Harrison. "Why can't we . . ."

"We've made our position clear," said Jason. "You must believe us when we say we can't teach you parapsychics. It's not something that can be taught. You must find it inside yourself. And you must believe us when we say we want nothing of technology. We people of this house have no need of it. The Indians dare not touch it, for it would ruin the kind of life they've fashioned. They live with nature, not on it. They take what nature gives; they do not rip their living out of nature. I can't speak for the robots, but I would suspect they have a technology of their own."

"There's one of them here," said Reynolds. "You need not speak for them."

"The one who is here," said Jason, "is more man than robot. He is doing mankind's work, has picked up something that we found too bulky or too inconvenient or not worthwhile to carry."

"We seek the truth," said Hezekiah. "We work for faith."

"This may all be true," Reynolds said to Jason, ignoring Hezekiah, "but there still remains your opposition to our resettling the Earth, colonizing it. There probably would not be many who would want to come, but you don't want even a few of us. You do not own the Earth. You cannot own it."

"Except for an emotional revulsion at seeing another technological threat to Earth," said Jason, "I don't suppose that Martha and myself could raise logical objection, and of this house, we are the only two who matter. The others are among the stars. When Martha and I are gone this house will stand empty and I know now there would be few, if any, who would really care. Earth has gone back to its primitive heritage and I would hate to see it stripped and gutted again. We did that to it once and once

should be enough. Earth should not stand in double
jeopardy. To me the matter is emotional, but there
are others, many others, to whom it really matters.
The Indians owned this continent once and the
whites took it from them. We slaughtered them and
robbed them and pushed them into reservations and
those who escaped the reservations we forced to live
in ghettos. Now they have made a new life, based
on the old—better than their old life because they
learned from us—but still their life, not ours. Neither
should they stand in double jeopardy. They should
be left alone."

"If we agreed," said Harrison, "to leave this continent alone, to only settle on the others . . ."

"In the old days," said Jason, "we made treaties
with the Indians. So long as the rivers flow, so long
as the winds shall blow, we said, the treaties would
be kept. They were never kept. And neither would
your so-called agreements. A few hundred years perhaps, more likely less than that. No longer. Even
from the first you would interfere. You'd want to set
up trade. You would break your old agreements and
then make new agreements and each time the Indian
would get less and less. It would be the same old
story as it was before. A technological civilization is
never satisfied. It is based on profit and progress, its
own brand of progress. It must expand or die. You
might make promises and be sincere in the making of
them; you might intend to keep them, but you
wouldn't and you couldn't."

"We would fight you," Red Cloud said. "We
would not want to fight, but we'd have to. We would
lose, we know that even now. But we still would
fight—once a plow was put into the ground, once
a tree was felled, once a wheel had turned . . ."

"You're insane!" shouted Harrison. "You are all
insane. You talk of fighting us! You? With spears
and arrows!"

"I told you," said Horace Red Cloud, "that we know we'd lose."

"And you close the planet to us," said Harrison, grimly, turning to Jason. "It's not your planet to close. It is ours as well as yours."

"The planet is not closed," said Jason. "We have no legal, perhaps not even a moral right to stand upon. But I ask you, in the name of common decency, to stay away from us, to keep your hands off us. You have other planets, there are still others you can take . . ."

"But this is our planet," Reynolds said. "It's been waiting all these years. You, a handful of people, can't keep the rest of the human race from taking what is theirs. We were taken from it; we did not desert it. All these years we have thought of it as home."

"You can't possibly expect us to believe that," said Jason. "Not the story of expatriates coming back, gratefully, to the old familiar shore. Let me tell you what I think."

"Yes, please do," said Reynolds.

"I think," said Jason, "that you may have known for years the location of the Earth, but you had no interest in it. You knew that it had little of value left, that it offered nothing but the room to live. And then, somehow, you heard a rumor about people left on Earth and how they could travel to the stars without any help at all—going anywhere they wished in the flicker of an eyelash—and how they talked telepathically across great distances. Perhaps not a true picture in the first rumor, but there were other rumors and the story built up and up. And you thought if only you could add this sort of ability to your technology you could progress the faster, that you'd increase your profits, that you'd have more power. And it wasn't until then that you thought of coming back to Earth."

"I fail to see the point of what you say," said Harrison. "The fact is we are here."

"The point is this," said Jason. "Don't use your threat to take over Earth in the belief that we are bluffing and will finally give in and give you what you want to keep you from colonizing Earth."

"And if we still decide to colonize?"

"Then you'll colonize. There's no way we can stop you. Red Cloud's people will be swept away. The robotic dream may end. Two cultures that might have come to something will be cut off and you'll have a worthless planet on your hands."

"Not worthless," Reynolds said. "You should give us credit for the progress we have made. With what we have now Earth would have economic value as an outpost, as a base, as an argicultural planet. It would be worth our while."

The candles guttered in a wind that came out of nowhere and a silence fell—a silence, Jason thought, because all had been said that could be said and there was no use of saying further. This was the end of it, he knew. There was no compassion in these two men across the table; an understanding, perhaps, of what might be at stake, but a cold, hard understanding that they'd weigh to their own advantage. They'd been sent to do a job, these two here and the others up there in the ship orbiting the Earth—they had been sent to do a job and they meant to do it. It did not matter to them what might come about because they did the job—it had never mattered, neither now nor in the years before. Societies had been smashed, cultures erased, human lives and hopes used up, all decency ignored. All was sacrificed to progress. And what, he wondered, might progress be? How did one define it? Was it merely naked power, or was there more to it than that?

Somewhere a door banged and a rush of chill autumn air came with the banging of the door. Feet

came down the hall and through the doorway came
a robot that glittered as he walked.

Jason came swiftly to his feet. "Stanley," he said,
"I'm glad that you could come, although I am afraid
too late."

Stanley gestured at the two across the table.

"Are these the ones?" he asked.

"They are, indeed," said Jason. "I would like to
have you meet . . ."

The robot brushed aside the introduction.

"Gentlemen," he said to them, "I have a message
for you."

32

He came down the ridge that ran above the river, striding in the crisp, moonlit autumn night, and came to the edge of a cornfield where the shocks stood like ghostly wigwams. Behind him the mewling creature humped along, hurrying to keep pace with him, tagging at his heels. From somewhere across the field a coon made lonesome whickering.

David Hunt was coming back to the great house that stood above the rivers; now he could come back because he knew the answer or at least the beginning of an answer. Evening Star would be waiting for him—at least, he hoped she would. He should, he realized, have told her of his going and the reason for it, but he'd not been able, for some reason he did not understand, to find the words and would have been embarrassed to speak even if he had known what to say.

He still carried the bow and the quiver of arrows was slung across his shoulder, although now he knew he carried them from habit; he no longer needed them. He wondered, as he strode along, how long he may have carried them beyond the time of need.

Above the trees he could see the topmost stories and the chimney-studded roof of the great house, a blur of darkness against the nighttime sky, and as he rounded a small tongue of timber that jutted out into the field, he saw the gleaming, metallic object that squatted there.

The sight of it brought him to a halt and he half crouched, as if the gleaming object might be an unknown danger, although even as he crouched, he knew what it was—a machine that brought men from the stars. Evening Star had told him of the threat posed to the Earth by such a ship that even then was heading toward the planet. And here it was; in the short time he'd been gone, it had arrived. But even so he felt a shiver of fear reach out and touch him and, touched by the fear, it seemed that he could see the indistinct outline of a shape that lurked behind the ship.

He moved backward a step and at the step, the shape moved out from behind the ship and it was strange that it should have been hidden by the ship, for it was larger than the ship. It was huge and, shadowy as it was, there was a brutality about it and as it lurched toward him he knew he had not outrun it, for all the miles he had covered. There was no outrunning it, he knew. He never should have tried.

The Dark Walker lurched another ponderous step and David turned to run, then spun back again to face the oncoming shadow-thing. If he ran now, he knew, he'd keep running and he would never quit. He'd go through life poised and set to run—as his people had run and run and run again.

Now, perhaps, there was no need to run.

It was closer now and he could see it better, although it bent forward, reaching for him, and the string came back, legs like tree trunks, a massive torso, a tiny head, clawed hands reaching out.

And in that moment it became, not the Dark Walker, but the grizzly bear rising from its bed and towering over him, too close to shoot, far too close to shoot. Without even thinking of it, his hand went back to grasp an arrow and the bow came up and his mind—or the thing inside his mind, the power inside his mind—went crashing out.

It did not drop as the grizzly had dropped. It faltered, bent forward, reaching for him, and the string came back, almost to the bowman's ear, with the arrow steady. The Walker dropped away and the arrow whistled and struck against the gleaming ship with a clanging sound. The Walker was no longer there.

David Hunt lowered the bow and stood shaking. He slumped to his knees and huddled, muscles twitching, nerves as taut as bowstrings. The can of worms moved closer to him, pressed hard against him, grew a tentacle and held him tight, broadcasting unheard comfort.

33

"Who is this person?" Reynolds asked Jason.

"His name is Stanley," Jason told him. "He is a robot from the Project. We told you of the Project, if you recall . . ."

"Oh, yes," said Harrison, "a superrobot being built by all his little brothers."

"I must protest your tone," said Hezekiah, sharply. "There is no reason for you to be supercilious. What this robot and his fellows do lies within the great tradition of your technology, to build bigger and better and with a greater imagination . . ."

"I beg your pardon," said Harrison. "But he came rushing in here . . ."

"He was invited," said Jason, coldly. "He had a long way to come. He has only now arrived."

"With a message?"

"It is from the Project," Stanley said.

"What is this message?" Harrison demanded.

"First I must explain it," said Stanley. "The Project, for some years now, has been in communication with intelligence somewhere in the central galaxy."

"Yes," said Reynolds. "We have been told of that."

"The message I carry," Stanley said, "is from that intelligence."

"And it has to do with the situation here?" asked Reynolds. "I find that ridiculous."

"It has to do with you," said Stanley.

"But how could it know? What would it know about the situation here? Certainly a great alien intelligence would not concern itself . . ."

"The message, directed to you and the rest of your party, is this: Leave Earth alone. No interference is allowed. It also is a part of the experiment."

"But I don't understand," Harrison said, angrily. "What experiment? What is it talking about? It makes no sense at all. Certainly, we have the right to know."

Stanley took a folded paper from a pouch. He tossed it across the table to Reynolds. "There is a copy of the message, off the printer."

Reynolds picked it up, glanced at it. "That is what it says. But I don't see the point. If you're trying another bluff . . ."

"It's the Principle," said Jason, speaking quietly. "That cinches it. We had wondered; now we know. The Project was talking with the Principle."

"A Principle?" yelled Harrison. "What is all this? We know of no Principle. It means nothing to us."

John sighed. "I don't suppose it does. We should have told you, but there was so much to tell. If you'll just settle back, I'll tell you about the Principle."

"Another fairy story, no doubt," Harrison said, angrily. "A phony message and now a fairy story. You people must think that we are stupid . . ."

"It doesn't matter now," said Jason. "It doesn't matter what you think. It's out of our hands entirely and it is out of yours."

John had been correct in his assumption, Jason told himself, that the people of the Earth had been made an experiment, in the same spirit and, perhaps, in much the same manner as a human bacteriologist or virologist would have experimented with a colony of bacteria or of virus. And if that were true, he realized with something of a shock, the people in this house and the little band of Indians and the other little group of people on the West Coast had not been missed. Rather, they deliberately had been left as a part of the experiment—as controls, perhaps.

John had said that by now the Principle would know that the strains of humanity ran true, but in the face of this new revelation, they must know as well that while in the mass humanity ran true, fragmented portions of it underwent mutation. For there were three human strains here—the people of this house and the Indians and the people on the coast. And of the three of them, two had been successful in their mutation and the third had gone to seed. Although, wait a minute, he told himself, that last conclusion is not true, for there was David Hunt. Thinking of him, he remembered how the music trees that evening of a week or two ago had suddenly regained their delicacy and poise and the incredible rumor he had heard from Thatcher this very afternoon. How was it, he wondered, the robots picked up the rumors before anyone else might be aware of them?

And the robots. Not three divergent strains, but four. Which was one up on the Principle, Jason thought with glee. He'd make any kind of bet (and be sure of winning) the Principle had not taken the robots into consideration. Although the robots, come to think of it, were a little frightening. What kind of contraption was this thing that could talk with the Principle and relay its message? And why had the Principle chosen it as spokesman? Simply because it had been there and handy? Or was there an affinity, an understanding, between the two of them that could not exist between the Principle and a human, or any other biologic form of life? He shivered at the thought of it.

"You remember," he said to Stanley, "that first you told us you could be of no help to us."

"I remember that," the robot said.

"But finally you were."

"I am very glad," said Stanley, "that we were able to help you in the end. You and we, I think, have very much in common."

"I sincerely hope we do," said Jason, "and I thank you from my heart."

34

She was sitting at the desk, with the books spread out, when he came into the room. For a moment, in the feeble candlelight, she could not be sure that it was he; then she saw it was. She came swiftly to her feet. "David!" she said.

He stood looking at her and she saw that he did not have the bow or the quiver of arrows. And something else as well—the necklace of bear claws no longer lay upon his chest. Silly, she thought, that she should notice things like that when all that really mattered was that he was back.

"The necklace," she said, feeling silly when she said it, not wanting to say it, but saying it just the same.

"I threw it away," he said.

"But, David . . ."

"I met the Walker. I did not need the bow. The arrow did not strike him; it only struck the ship."

She did not answer.

"You thought the Walker was only a shadow in my mind."

"Yes," she said. "A piece of folklore. An olden story . . ."

"Perhaps it was," he said. "I don't know. Perhaps a shadow of that great race of builders who once lived here. The people not like us. Not like you and I. The shadow that they cast upon the land, that even after they were gone still remained upon the land."

"A haunt," she said. "A ghost."

"But it is gone now," he said. "It no longer walks."

She stepped around the desk and he came quickly to meet her and had his arms about her and held her close against him. "It is so strange about the two of us," he said. "I can make things well, I can cure the sick. You can see everything there is and make me see it, too; everything there is comes clear inside your mind."

She did not answer. He was too close, too real; he was back again. There was no room for answer.

But, within her mind, she told Grandfather Oak: It is a new beginning . . .

"I'll be leaving soon," said John. "I won't remain away so long this time."

"I hate to see you go," said Jason. "Do come back as soon as you are able. We were boys together . . ."

"We had good times," said John.

"There is something very special," Jason said, "about two men being brothers."

"There is nothing to worry over now," said John. "The Earth is safe. We can continue as we have. The Indians and the robots can take any road they wish. The idea of the Principle may not be accepted in its entirety by the People. They'll think about it for a while, they'll mull it over, they'll talk it over. They'll figure, as Harrison said, it probably is no more than a fairy tale. They may make a try for Earth. I would think it's almost certain that they will. If they do, they'll get slapped down and then they will believe."

Jason nodded. "That is true. But there's the business of the Project."

"What about the Project?"

"You mean you haven't thought of it?"

"You're talking riddles, Jason."

"No, I'm not," said Jason. "It's just that you haven't seen it. No one saw it. They figured all the Principle did was use the Project for an errand boy."

"Well, wasn't that what it was—now, wait a second, you can't be thinking . . ."

"But I am," said Jason. "Not an errand boy for the Principle, but a spokesman for the Principle. What have the two in common? We wondered whether the Project might just be listening, but now we know it wasn't that. They were talking back and forth. The Project told the Principle what was going on and the Principle told it what to do . . ."

"I think you may be right," said John, "but you must remember that we've met other intelligences and we've had slight success . . ."

"The thing you don't realize," said Jason, "is that the Principle is not another alien, not just another intelligence you run into out in space. It could have talked to us, I think, to any one of us, if it had wanted to."

John grunted. "That raises a question, Jason. Like speaks to like. Would you suppose the Principle could be—no, it can't be that. It must be something else. The Principle is no machine. I can swear to that. I lived on the edge of it for days."

"That's not the point," said Jason. "The Principle would have nothing to do with a mere machine. Could it be, I wonder, that the Project is no longer a machine? How far do you have to push a machine before it becomes something other than machine? How much does a machine need to evolve before it becomes something else—another form of life? Different than we are, it would have to be different than we are, but a life form just as surely . . ."

"You're letting your imagination run away with you," said John. "Even if you aren't, there's nothing we need fear. The robots are friends of ours. They have to be good friends—damn it, man, we made them."

"I don't think it's all imagination," Jason said. "I think there is some basis for it, some evidence of it. I find myself wondering if the Principle, whatever it may be, has found a closer identification with the Project than it has with the human race. And that's the kind of thing that sends a shiver up my spine."

"Even if it should be so," said John, "and I can't agree it is, it would make no difference to us. Except for you and Martha, we're out among the stars. In another few thousand years there'll be none of us who'll care particularly either about the Principle or Earth. We're free agents, going where we want to go, doing what we want to do. And this business of star-roving, I feel sure, is only a part of it, a beginning of it. In the centuries to come the race will develop other capabilities. I don't know what they'll be, but I know they will develop."

"I may be short-sighted," Jason admitted. "I live too close to Earth. I never gained the perspective the others of you have. By the time the situation with the Project has developed to the point where it has any impact, Martha and I will be long gone. But the Indians will stay here and what about the Indians? Of all of us, they may be the most important segment of the human race."

John chuckled. "The Indians will get along all right. They've developed the most solid basis of any of us. They've made a compact with the planet. They've become a part of it."

"I hope," said Jason, "you are right."

They sat in silence, the fire flickering in the grate, the chimney making sighing noises. The wind plucked at the eaves and in the stillness of the night the old house moaned with its weight of years.

Finally John said, "There's one thing I want to know and I want the truth. What about your alien?"

"It left," said Jason. "It went home. It stayed longer than it planned because it had to tell someone, had to thank someone. David was the man to thank, for David was the one who did it, but David never heard a single word it said. So it came to me and told me."

"And you've told David? You passed along the thanks?"

Jason shook his head. "No, not yet. If ever. He's not ready for it. It might frighten him. He might run off again. I told two people, you and Hezekiah."

John frowned. "Was it smart to tell Hezekiah?"

"I debated it," said Jason, "then finally I did. It seemed—well, it seemed to be in his department. He's so weighed down with imaginary, self-accusatory worry, that I thought it might help him. Give him something solid to worry over for a change."

"This wasn't really what I meant," said John, "when I asked the question. What worries me is this matter of a soul. Do you honestly think it possible this strange character out of the West could have given the alien a soul?"

"That's what the alien said."

"Not the alien. You. What do you think?"

"I sometimes think," said Jason, "that the soul may be a state of mind."

Hezekiah tramped, troubled, up and down the garden of the monastery.

It was impossible, he told himself, that what Mr. Jason told him could be right. Mr. Jason must have misunderstood. He wished the alien still were here, so that he could talk with it, although Mr. Jason has said, even had it been here, he could not talk with it. There was no way for him to talk with it.

The night was silent and the stars far off. A winter wind came stealing up an autumn hill. Hezekiah shivered at the touch of it and was at once disgusted with himself and a little frightened. He should not shiver in the wind, he could not feel the wind. Could it be, he wondered, that he was turning human? Could he, in his humanness, really feel the wind?

And he was even more frightened that he should think he might be human than he'd been frightened at shivering in the wind.

Pride, he thought—pride and vanity. Would he ever rid himself of his pride and vanity? And he might as well admit it—when would he be rid of doubt?

And now, as he asked himself that question, he could no longer hide from the thing he had been hiding from, the thought he had tried to keep himself from facing by thinking about the alien and its soul.

The Principle!

"No!" he shouted at himself, in sudden terror. "No, it can't be so! There can be nothing to it. It is sacrilege to even think of it."

In that area, he fiercely reminded himself, he could not be shaken.

God must be, forever, a kindly old (human) gentleman with a long, white, flowing beard.

ABOUT THE AUTHOR

Clifford D. Simak was born and raised in southwestern Wisconsin, a land of wooded hills and deep ravines which he often uses as the background locale for his stories. Over the years he has written over 25 books, and he has some 200 short stories to his credit. In 1977, Simak was awarded the Nebula Grand Master by the Science Fiction Writers of America. A retired newspaperman, Simak and his wife Kay live in Minnesota. They have two children. His most recent novel, also published by Del Rey Books, is PROJECT POPE.